To Adella,

You are a blessing
to me. I love you
with the love of Jesus!

Nobody's Business

God Bless you!

Author: Rebecca Simmons
Published by: Diligence Publishing Company

Published by: Diligence Publishing Company, 41 Watchung Plaza, #239, Montclair, New Jersey 07042

Front cover design: Olson Jean-Louis, Illustrator and Graphic Artist

Cover Illustration
Copyright © 2003 by
Diligence Publishing

Author Photo: Maureen Arscott

ISBN: 0-9727416-0-7

Printed in the United States by
Morris Publishing
3212 East Highway 30
Kearney, NE 68847
1-800-650-7888

Visit the publisher's website at www.dpc-books.com

Dedications

This book is dedicated to my mother, who always put her children's needs in front of her own. I am forever grateful for her sacrifices and her unconditional love; to the loving memory of Mr. Wavie, who always encouraged me to do my very best and to keep it as real as I possibly can; to my sisters and brother, who listened to my stories and encouraged me to live my dreams; to my oldest daughter, who loves me in spite of my shortcomings as a mother while she was growing up; finally, to my wonderful husband, Anthony (the fuel in my tank), who never complained about the times that he had to wash clothes, feed the kids and clean the house while I was writing this book. These people have shown me countless examples of what it means to really love someone.

Acknowledgements

First and foremost, I would like to thank God for giving me the inspiration and ability to write this book. I would like to thank my husband, Anthony, for standing patiently by my side and covering for me around the house while I worked on this project. I would also like to thank him for loving me and accepting me for who God made me to be. I would like to thank my children, Kayla, Marcus, and Justin for allowing me time out when they may have wanted more of my attention. I would like to thank my first born, Hakida, for loving me so much and believing that her mom could do this.

I would like to thank my mother and my father for bringing me into the world and for being the best parents that they knew how to be. I want to especially thank my mother for cooking all of those Sunday dinners and always loving me even when I thought I was unlovable. I would like to acknowledge my sisters, all of them, for putting up with me all of these years. I would like to thank my oldest sister, Janice, for teaching me how to fight for what is right. I would like to thank my sister, Rasheedah, for her love and her encouragement. I would especially like to thank my sister, Jacki, for always being such an inspiration to me. Her strength, courage and diligence in everything she endeavored have always prompted me to try to keep up with her. A special acknowledgement goes out to my baby sister, Renee, who has a heart of gold and has always looked up to me as her big sister, even when I didn't deserve it. I thank my one and only brother, Gary, for always believing in me and keeping me out of trouble when I was a young girl. I would like to thank him and his lovely wife, Vonda (another one of my sisters), for promoting "Nobody's Business" to the hilt in Virginia.

I would like to acknowledge all of my friends at Merrill Lynch, who provoked me to do more and to be more, but especially Julita Romano, who taught me how to be a lady and gave me the wise advice on who to marry. She told me to "Marry a man who loves you more than you love him." It took me awhile to realize that this advice was as good as gold.

I would like to thank all of my friends who have cheered me on through the years. I would like to especially thank my girls, Cathy Griggs and Audrey Swinson. I believe that God placed these two women in my life for such a time as this. Cathy is always there when I need words of wisdom or a prayer, and Audrey has been my biggest encourager over the years. She has stood beside me and cheered me on each time that I have stepped out to live my dreams.

Special thanks go out to Carmela Frequenza and Kathy Harris for reading my manuscript and critiquing it and helping me to edit it. Without these two ladies, I don't know how I would have gotten through the tedious task of editing this book.

With a heart of gratitude, I acknowledge the marriage ministry at The Cathedral International for their friendship and their prayers. This group of people is very special indeed and I love them. Finally, last but certainly not least, I would like to give thanks to my church family: to my Pastor, Dr. Donald Hilliard Jr., who has poured into my life with his whole heart and soul for the past nine years. It was through reading his books that I was inspired to go after my dream of being a writer; to my first lady, Minister Phyllis, who has been my example of what it is to be a lady; to my Pastor, Dr. Bernadette Glover-Williams, who once told me that I didn't need a sugar daddy, but that God would take care of all of my needs; to Pastor Patricio Wilson, who taught me that it's okay to cry and let God heal my pain; to Pastor Dr. Denise Reid, who told me that I didn't have to live with a bad relationship, but that with God, there is an awesome kind of love; to Bill and Bebe Major, who have always embraced me with hearts of love; to Thomas and Leslie Lukoma, who have shown me what it means to have real faith; and to all of my brothers and sisters at The Cathedral International, who love on me week after week and help me to know that I am wonderfully and fearfully made, I say thank you, thank you, thank you and I love you.

A special acknowledgement goes out to my new friends at Several Sources. You ladies have shown me what it means to be courageous and to have faith when it seems like the odds are against you. Keep the faith and keep pressing towards your dreams.

The Crisis Center

Clara sat at her desk looking at the young woman seated across from her. She sighed as she realized that this session would end like all of the others. She gazed through the panes of the windows of her office, wishing that she could escape the madness of the center. Then she absentmindedly scribbled the word impossible on her pad and glanced over at Patricia again.

Patricia had been crying for the last ten minutes and she would cry harder and louder each time Clara tried to get her to talk about what was causing her so much pain.

Clara wondered what on earth could be so hard for the woman to face. She couldn't figure it out. Clara didn't know how to help Patricia. All she did know was that she was ready to go.

Clara inhaled and exhaled. Then she got up and walked around to the front of the desk. Sitting on the edge of her desk, she leaned ever so slightly towards Patricia. "Come on, Patricia. Talk it out. You've got to keep talking to me." Clara tried again to help Patricia to face the thing that was hurting her so much, although deep inside she felt that it was hopeless. Patricia seemed to be holding on tightly to her pain, shielding it like a prized possession.

"No. I can't," Patricia wailed. "It hurts too much. I can't talk about it. Not now. Not ever!"

"Well, then Patricia," Clara said as she moved around the desk to sit in her chair. "I think we should end our session for today."

Clara was really having a hard time dealing with Patricia today. She had been seeing her for three months now. Sometimes it seemed they were making progress, but things always came to a grinding halt each time Clara tried to get Patricia to talk about her childhood. Clara looked at Patricia again and wondered what she could do to help her to deal with this thing that was hurting her so much. She couldn't figure out why Patricia kept coming to the Center. She acted like she wanted help, but she refused to cooperate with Clara. Clara knew no more about her than she did on the first day that she came in. Clara leaned back in her chair. She closed her eyes for a moment and then took another long look at her client. She remembered the day when Patricia had first come into the Center.

Clara was standing in the reception area talking to two of the other counselors who worked there. Patricia walked in slowly, looking behind her as if she was afraid she was being followed. They all stopped in mid conversation to turn and stare at her. The woman looked like she had just been in a fight for her life. She had bruises all over her. She wore shorts and a torn T-shirt. She had a black eye and scratches and black and blue marks all over her arms and legs. She was really in bad shape. The three counselors rushed over to help her. They took her into Clara's office, and after she was settled, they left her there with Clara. Clara wondered why she always ended up with the stragglers. Most of them disillusioned and hurt just like this woman. Perhaps it was because her office was closest to the door, or maybe it was just chance. "Do you want me to call the police?" She reached over and picked up the phone. Patricia's eyes filled with naked fear. She looked like a deer caught in the headlights of an oncoming car, and Clara immediately knew that this was another woman who would not report her abuser. In the months to follow, Patricia came in over and over again with black eyes and bruises, and each time she refused to turn her husband in.

"Okay. I've had enough for one day," Clara thought as she picked up her pen. She made a couple of notations on the patient sheet and handed it to Patricia.

"Okay, Patricia. You can give this to the girl at the front desk, and I'll see you in two weeks."

Patricia reached for the patient sheet and Clara noticed that her hand was trembling.

"Patricia, why are you shaking?" Clara asked. "Did something happen? Do you want to talk about it?"

Patricia looked at Clara with a scared, confused look on her face. Then she blurted out, "Brian thinks we should have a baby."

Clara clenched her fists around the pen in her hand and took a deep breath. Her heartbeat quickened at the thought of these two mixed up people having a baby.

"He wants us to start trying to get pregnant." Patricia spoke as if in a daze.

"You don't want to bring a baby into this mess, do you?" Clara asked wondering if Patricia would be crazy enough to get pregnant.

Patricia shook her head. "I don't know if I want to have children at all."

"Good," Clara thought as she exhaled. She realized that she had been holding her breath.

"Only Brian doesn't know about that." Patricia's shoulders slumped as she sat there looking helpless. "He says if I love him, I'll have his baby."

"You and Brian have to get yourselves together before you think about having a baby."

Patricia looked like she wanted to say something. She opened her mouth as if to speak but no words came out. Then she slumped back against the couch with tears flowing down her face.

Clara went on. "You know, Patricia, you don't have to live like this. Why do you stay with him when he beats you all the time? And why would you even consider having his baby?"

Patricia reached over to take some tissue from the box that Clara was extending to her. "You'll never understand." She wiped her tears and nose with the tissue. Then she looked up at Clara. Her eyes were glazed as if she was in a trance.

Clara wondered if Brian was practicing some type of voodoo magic or something.

Patricia interrupted her thoughts. "Brian and I love each other. Sure he beats me. But he says he's going to stop. Besides, it's mostly my fault. None of this would happen if I would just do what I'm supposed to do."

Clara wanted to scream. She had heard this story before. Women came into the center half dead and then they blamed themselves for the fact that some man had taken the liberty to beat the heck out of them. Clara wondered how Brian had convinced Patricia that his beating her up was her fault. Clara was almost convinced that it was some kind of black magic.

"Patricia, it's not your fault," she told the woman for what seemed like the thousandth time. Clara had to force herself not to sound impatient. How could Patricia think that she deserved to be beaten? "No one deserves to be beaten." At that moment, Clara wished that she could shake some sense into Patricia, but at the same time her heart went out to the woman.

"Yes, it is my fault. Brian said he wouldn't beat me if I didn't make him do it." She sniffled again and blew her nose into the tissue. "It's just that I make him so mad sometimes. I leave him no choice but to hit me. I just have to try harder to be a good wife and not to make him so angry all the time."

Clara stood up and walked over to the couch where Patricia was sitting. She sat down and reached for Patricia's hands. Holding her hands in hers, she asked, "Patricia, tell me, do you really think you deserve to be beaten by Brian or anyone else for that matter?"

"I...I have to go." Patricia jumped up and picked up her purse. Clutching it close to her chest, she looked wildly around the room as if looking for a way to escape.

Clara stared sadly at Patricia who looked like she wanted to run. Why couldn't she get Patricia to see that Brian didn't love her? She remembered her mother telling her that no man should hit a woman, especially if he loved her. Slowly she got up from the couch and took a step in Patricia's direction. "Do you really think that being punched and slapped around is love?" Clara refused to give up. "Does love mean that you allow yourself to be thrown down and kicked?"

"Clara, I just don't know anymore." Patricia seemed to have calmed down a little. She stood there face to face with Clara. Her eyes begged Clara to understand. "All I can tell you is that I love my husband, and I don't want to lose him. He just gets so mad..."

Clara rested her hands lightly on Patricia's shoulders and looked into her worn face. "Okay. Okay," she interrupted her. "You say that you don't want to lose Brian, but would you rather lose your life?"

Patricia shook herself free of Clara's grasp and squared her shoulders. "Listen," she hissed. "I didn't come here for you to tell me to leave my husband." Her lips curled as she snarled angrily at Clara. "I told you. I love him. He is the only one who would want..." Her voice trailed off as she stopped in mid sentence all of a sudden lost in thought.

Clara studied her face waiting for her to finish. Patricia looked angry and confused at the same time. Clara couldn't figure it out. Why was Patricia mad at her? She was just trying to help. She should be mad at the jerk that keeps beating her up. Patricia had gone from hysterics to sadness, to anger, to hostility – all in one session today. But the look that Clara saw on her face now was one of anger mixed with fear and utter dismay. Clara wondered again what was really eating Patricia. What could make her want to stay with a man like Brian? "The only one who would want what, Patricia?"

Patricia was so lost in her thoughts that she jumped at the sound of Clara's voice.

Clara watched as a look of determination crossed Patricia's face and she knew that she had lost her.

Patricia clutched her purse tighter and glanced at the door. "I have to go," she said quickly as she rushed to the door, opened it, and left the room before Clara could stop her.

Clara shook her head slowly from side to side as she stood looking at the open door. She glanced down at the couch and realized that Patricia had left the patient sheet. She picked it up and walked slowly to her desk where she sat down to make a couple of notations on the sheet. As she wrote, she wondered what it would take for Patricia to realize that she was in danger of being killed. Clara had tried to tell her. Men like Brian didn't stop beating their women until it was too late, but Patricia never seemed to be listening to her. She refused to hear the facts about men who beat up on women or the statistics about the lives that were lost. Clara gazed across the room, wondering if Patricia would ever leave Brian. She hoped that Patricia would wake up and smell the coffee before she ended up in the morgue. She got up and took the patient sheet to her secretary, who was sitting right outside her office.

"Here is the patient sheet on Patricia Walker," she told her secretary as she looked around at the women in the waiting room. "How many more people do I have to see today?"

Sandra flipped through the appointment book and looked at the walk-in sheet before she answered. "Just one more," she told her boss while looking around the almost empty waiting room. "This is her first time here. She wouldn't tell me what the problem was."

"Where is she?" Clara scanned the room with her eyes, wondering which one of the women seated there was going to be her next client.

"Well, that's just it," Sandra said. "She was sitting right there waiting." Sandra pointed at an empty chair. "She seemed to be a little nervous and then her cell phone rang. She sounded annoyed at the person on the phone, and then she walked over and told me she had to leave for a few minutes. She said she'd be back." Sandra shrugged her shoulders. "I've been so busy that I never noticed that she didn't come back. I just assumed she had."

"Well, I hope she hurries up," Clara sulked. "I need to get out of here." She looked at her watch and then back at Sandra. "Maybe she won't come back. Either way, if she's not back by 5:00, she'll have to catch me on another day."

Sandra looked up at her. "Are you okay? You look like you're having a rough day."

"I am! I don't know what it is, but seeing Patricia always takes a lot out of me." Clara tilted her head to the side and rubbed her neck. "She comes in here every two weeks, but we never get anywhere." Still rubbing her neck, she rolled her head from side to side and then she looked straight at Sandra with glazed eyes. "She lets that husband of hers beat the mess out of her and then she comes in here just to cry on my shoulder." Clara's eyes were misty. She looked down at her shoes as she tried to hold back the tears. Still looking at her feet she said, "I just don't know how much more of this I can take."

Sandra just sat there shaking her head as she watched Clara.

Clara looked up at Sandra. "What are you sitting there shaking your head at me for?" Clara's voice trembled and she realized that she was crying.

"Are you forgetting?" Sandra rolled her eyes. "This is a women's crisis center. You're a counselor. That means you get to listen to people's problems."

Clara laughed as she sniffled and wiped away the two tears that were rolling down each side of her face. "Yeah, I know. I just wonder sometimes if I'm helping anybody. They walk out of here with the same problems that they walk in with. Week after week. Month after month. Nothing seems to change." She sighed. Then she took a deep breath and tried to regain her composure. "Sometimes I wonder if I'm even in the right business."

Clara really cared about the women that came into the Center. But counseling these women was taking its toll on her. She came to the Center every day ready to take on the world and make a difference, and she left this place every day, disappointed and discouraged. No one ever thanked her for taking on their burdens and most of the time, her clients got mad at her for telling them the truth about their situations. Clara wanted to quit sometimes but she couldn't. She had a fire in her heart to help these women. She couldn't abandon them.

"Yeah, your job is tough. I wouldn't take it for all the money in the world." Sandra made no bones about the fact that she wouldn't want to be in Clara's shoes.

"It's not even the money." Clara looked around the waiting room at the few women there. "It's just that these women have so many problems. I wish I could help."

"Well, I have enough problems of my own. The last thing I want to do is sit around and listen to other people's problems." Sandra reached over to answer the ringing phone.

Clara didn't know why she did it either. It wasn't as if she also didn't have problems of her own. While she waited for Sandra to get off the phone, she thought about her boyfriend and her mother and sister. Although she hated to think about it, she sure did have her own problems. She was having problems in her relationship with Jason, and her mother and sister were driving her nuts. She secretly hoped that dealing with the other women's problems would somehow help her to deal with her own. So far that strategy was getting her nothing but more aggravation and heartache. Clara became so attached to the women at the Center that their business became her business, heaping on to the heavy load that she already carried. Clara's back ached from carrying the weight of the world on her shoulders for the past two years.

Sandra hung up the phone and looked up at Clara who was standing there slumped over like she was carrying a heavy load. She was almost tilted to the side with this strange look on her face. Sandra got up and walked over to her. "Hey. Are you okay?"

Clara looked at Sandra with a blank look on her face. Then she snapped out of it. "I just don't know why I come in here day after day," Clara spoke her thoughts out loud, repeating the familiar dialogue once again. "Besides, you're right. It's not as if I don't have enough problems of my own." She headed towards her office before Sandra could answer her. She stopped at the door and turned around. "Listen, if that woman comes back, just give her to someone else. I have to get out of here." She went into her office and closed the door behind her.

The Park

Ten minutes later, Clara left the Center. She stood on the sidewalk and breathed deeply of the fresh air. It felt good to be outside. She realized that she had been cramped up in that building all day. She hadn't even gone out for lunch, but had ordered a soup and salad to be delivered. And when it arrived, she ate in her office. She took another deep breath of the fresh air. Then she walked over to her car and opened the door. She smiled as she slid into the comfortable, plush leather interior of the BMW that she had bought for her birthday this year. She started the engine and put the car in drive, turning on the radio as she pulled out of the parking lot into the afternoon traffic. The sweet sounds of jazz flooded the interior of Clara's car. The trumpet notes bounced off of the windows and wrapped themselves around Clara as she drove. Clara loved jazz. Anytime she wanted to escape, she would put on some jazz. The trumpets were her favorite. "What a sexy sounding instrument," Clara thought as she cruised and let herself get lost in the music.

As Clara turned the corner close to her house, the music faded into the background of the sudden sense of dread that crept into her entire being. Suddenly, she realized that she didn't want to go home. She pictured Jason sitting there, waiting for her and the feeling of dread intensified. They argued a lot lately, and she wasn't in the mood for a fight tonight. She wished that she had someplace else to go, but she didn't. She didn't have any real friends. All she had was Jason and work. She could go to her mother's. But that wasn't an option that she'd consider since she really didn't like going there either.

As Clara got even closer to home, she made a left turn into the park that was around the corner from her house. She parked under a tree and watched the children playing on the swings in the distance. Clara rolled down her windows so she could hear their laughter. They looked like they were having fun. Clara remembered when she was a kid and she and her sister would come to this same park to play.

They would run and swing and laugh and play all day until it got dark. Then they would head home where their parents would be waiting for them. She remembered how she dreaded going home then too. Often, she and her sister got in trouble for staying at the park too long. But most of the time, her parents were too drunk to notice. They usually had company over and would be drinking, playing cards and listening to loud music. They would shoo them into the other room so that they could continue to entertain their friends. Her sister, who was three years older than she was, would fix their dinner. After they ate dinner, they would sit on the beds in their room and talk until they fell asleep, dirty and exhausted.

Clara opened the compartment in between the seats and pulled out the fifth of vodka that she kept there. She opened the bottle and poured some into a cup. Then she put some tonic in from the bottle under her seat and stirred it with her finger. She took a swig and wrinkled her nose at the taste. Boy, that was a strong drink and it could use some ice. But Clara was used to drinking without ice. She didn't care about the taste anyway. She just wanted to hurry up and feel some relief from this awful feeling that she had. She finished the drink and poured another one. She looked around at the leaves of the trees rustling in the cool summer's breeze. She got out of the car and walked over to the water, making sure to take her booze with her. The park was so peaceful. Clara sat down on the grass and tucked her legs beneath her. She watched the ducks swimming in the water as she listened to the sounds of joy coming from the children in the playground area off in the distance. She loved the park. When she was in the park, she forgot about all of her problems. Sitting under the rustling leaves, she dreamed about a different life, and the voices in her head disappeared as she watched the children play. She always imagined that she was someone else. Not the messed up counselor who couldn't even get her own life together, let alone help other people. But she didn't want to think about her problems right now. After all, she was in the park. The park was sacred ground. It was the closest that she got to God and nothing was going to interfere with that. Clara dreamed about how life could be as she poured herself another drink. "Just one more drink," she told herself. "Just one more drink and then I'll go home."

But Clara didn't go home. She sat in the park until she finished the whole bottle. Clara held the empty bottle up and looked inside. "Gone," she slurred drunkenly as she threw the bottle into the lake. She giggled as she looked around to see if anyone had seen her. "Oops," she said, putting her hand to her mouth as if to hide a secret. Wobbly, she stood to her feet and stumbled over to her car. It seemed to take forever to open the car door. The world started to spin and she couldn't get the key in the lock. Clara wished the car would stop moving. That was the only thing she didn't like about her stupid car. She was in no mood for this little game. She felt horrible. If she could just get in and sit down for a few minutes, everything would be all right. "Thank you!" she said as she yanked the car door open and crawled inside. As she sat in the driver's seat, she felt dizzy and the world started spinning even faster, then faster. Before she knew what happened, she passed out.

....

Clara woke up with her head buried in the passenger seat. She sat up and looked around her.

"God, my head hurts," she thought as she reached up and held her head with both hands. She sat back and put her head against the headrest until the throbbing in her head eased a little. Slowly, she looked around again and realized that she was still in the park. Everything was dark and she could hear the crickets chirping through the open window. The little children had all gone home. Clara's car was the only one there. She looked at her watch. She had been here for over two hours. Clara let out a sigh of relief. She was lucky that no one had mugged her or, worse, raped her. What was her problem? How could she get drunk and pass out in the park? But this was not the first time. Clara was trying to stop drinking so much. But she was never happy until the bottle was empty. This had been happening a lot lately. No wonder she and Jason fought so much. He couldn't figure out where she disappeared to all the time, and she couldn't bring herself to tell him. What would he think about that? If he knew she was a drunk? She couldn't let him find out. Nobody had to know. She should probably get some help. No, she could stop on her own. All she had to do was make up her mind and she could stop. "Okay. This was the last time," Clara swore to herself as she slumped over the steering wheel, blinded by the pain in her head. "Once I sober up this time, I'll never drink again," she vowed as she rolled up her windows. She locked her doors and slumped across the front seat of her car. "If I can just close my eyes for a few minutes, I'll be okay. If I can just get through this," she thought to herself. "If I can just make it through this, I'll never

17

get drunk again," she promised herself as she drifted off to sleep again.

Jason

Two hours later, Clara woke up and looked at her watch. Nine o'clock. She had to get home. She knew that Jason would be wondering where she was. She sat up and groaned at the throbbing pain that was still pounding in her head. She felt like her head was going to burst open, splattering her brains all over the place. What was she thinking? Drinking that whole bottle of liquor. "Oh well," she thought as she pulled down the visor to look in the mirror. At least she had slept most of it off. She ran her fingers through her hair. She looked horrible. Her eyes were bloodshot, and her mascara was streaked. She must have been crying again. She seemed to be crying a lot lately. She tried to figure out why as she pulled out her compact and fixed her makeup. Then she put some Clearzine in her eyes. "Thank God for Clearzine," Clara thought as she put the car in drive and headed home.

Clara pulled into the driveway behind Jason's silver Acura. Her heart beat faster as she wondered what kind of mood he would be in tonight. He had been sulking a lot lately. Clara couldn't figure out what was wrong with him. She just knew that she was tired of him sulking around all the time, acting like a spoiled little boy. She couldn't stand him lately. Clara couldn't believe that she used to be crazy about him. They used to laugh and play silly games and Clara had felt like the luckiest woman in the world to have him in her life. Now, all they did was argue and fight all the time. Clara wondered why he even stayed with her. Clara had her ways and she wasn't about to change them. After all, she didn't know where she would begin to change or how to change for that matter. So she thought it was better not to bother. Jason could either take her like she was or leave her alone. She was fine before she met him and she would be just fine without him. Clara felt strong as she squared her shoulders and braced herself to go into the house.

"Oh well, here goes nothing," she said softly as she popped a mint into her mouth and inhaled deeply. Exhaling and inhaling a couple more times, she let out the last breath and reached for the door handle. She stepped out of the car and marched towards the house. Maybe she'd get lucky tonight. Maybe he'd be downstairs in the basement working out on the exercise equipment that they both loved to use. This would give her a chance to run upstairs to brush her teeth and freshen up her breath. As she put the key in the door, she hoped that Jason would be asleep or something. She entered the house and walked into the kitchen. Her heart sank when she saw Jason sitting at the table going through some mail. He looked up when she came into the room.

"Hi, honey." He greeted her warmly, smiling as he got up from the table to give her a kiss.

Clara kept moving towards the living room and started up the stairs before he could get to her. "I have to go to the bathroom," she called back to Jason as she ran up the steps. "I'll be right back down." She went into the bathroom and locked the door. Leaning against the door, she let out a sigh of relief. She waited a couple of minutes for her heart to slow down. Then she walked over to the sink. She looked in the mirror and frowned at her appearance. How could Jason love her? She looked horrible with deep dark circles under her eyes and her hair matted from her nap in the car. After she brushed her teeth and gargled with mouthwash, she popped another mint into her mouth. Then she washed her face and freshened her makeup. After combing her hair, she smiled at the girl in the mirror. "That's a lot better," she said as she winked at her reflection. "Okay, now let's get out here and see what happens next." She unlocked the door and grabbed the doorknob to let herself out of the bathroom.

She walked into the bedroom and started making her bed. She woke up late this morning, and the bedroom was a mess. She couldn't make up her mind what to wear to work today and her clothes were thrown all over the place. After she had finally decided on an outfit to wear, she had to search to find the shoes to go with it. So, one by one she had thrown all of the shoes out of the closet and left them wherever they landed. She knew that Jason hated it when she left the bedroom like this, but she just couldn't bring herself to get up any earlier. Because she waited until the last possible minute to get out of her bed, she was always rushing to get ready and never had time to make the bed before going to work. That wouldn't be so bad if she didn't change clothes two or three times each morning before leaving the house, pulling off dresses and suits and throwing them on the bed, the dresser, and sometimes even the floor. She and Jason argued all the time because he felt that she should be neater. He was sure getting on her nerves lately. She didn't know that he was such a neat freak until they moved in together.

"Hey, I thought you were coming back down."

Clara jumped at the sound of Jason's voice.

Jason walked into the room and came over to kiss her. "You smell like mouthwash." He backed up from her and wrinkled his nose.

Clara felt herself getting upset. She hated when Jason did that. What was the deal with him? Always sniffing on her like he was a search dog or something. "Oh. I had garlic for lunch and it was driving me nuts," she lied trying hard not to lose her temper. "I also had a drink and that sure didn't mix too well with the garlic."

Jason arched his eyebrow in the disapproving way that drove Clara crazy. "You had a drink?" He squinted his eyes the way he always did when he was getting ready to interrogate her.

Clara knew what was coming next. He was going to tell her that he didn't like for her to drink when he wasn't around. He had seen her drunk a few times, and the last time he had told her that he didn't think she could handle her liquor.

"You know that you can't handle too much alcohol." Jason sounded agitated. "I hope you only had one drink."

Clara's temper flared. She couldn't hold back any longer. "Jason, you're not my father and you're definitely not my boss!" she hissed. "I can have a drink, or two, or three if I want to!" she yelled at him at the top of her lungs staring at him as if daring him to say another word.

Jason held up his hands and backed up a couple of steps. "Hey, wait a minute. I only meant that you get a little crazy when you drink too much."

Clara was not backing down. "Well Mister, you said too much. I'm a grown woman, and if I want to drink, I will!" she replied huffily as she stormed past him towards the door.

"Clara, come on now. Wait a minute." Jason reached out and pulled her to him. "Is everything okay? You only drink when something is bothering you." He held her close and stroked her hair. "Do you want to talk about what's going on with you lately?" His voice was filled with concern.

"No. I don't need you to counsel me," Clara said flippantly, pushing against his chest. "Remember, I'm the counselor, not you."

She spoke in such a nasty tone that Jason let her go. He stared at her for a moment, then turned and headed out of the room.

Clara reached out and grabbed his shirt. She pulled him back into the room so hard they both fell on the bed. "Now, where do you think you're going?" she slurred drunkenly. "You always start the fight and then you want to walk out on me." She rolled over on him and straddled him with her legs.

"Clara, just as I thought." Jason pushed her off of him. "You're drunk."

"Drunk? Drunk?" Clara scrambled up from where she had landed when Jason pushed her. She tried to compose herself as she stood at the edge of the bed. "Who are you calling drunk?" Clara wanted to shut up, but she couldn't. "You think you're so smart," she slurred. "I'm not drunk."

Jason tried to get up from the bed.

Clara pushed him back down. "I told you. You're not going anywhere." She stood over him with her hands on her hips.

"Listen," Jason said standing up. He moved quickly away from Clara, holding his hands up as if to keep her away from him. "I need to go downstairs and cool off for a minute."

"No," Clara told him. "You started this and you're going to stay until it's finished."

Jason shook his head. He looked around the room as if looking for a way out.

"And don't go shaking your head at me."

Jason held up his finger and pointed at Clara. Looking her square in the eye, he scolded her. "Clara, you're drunk. And I refuse to deal with you when you're like this."

Clara opened her mouth to respond but thought better of it. She stood there trying to think of something to say.

Jason walked over to the closet and took out his jacket. He turned towards Clara and studied her as he put first one arm and then the other through the sleeves of the jacket. Then he walked towards the door. "I'm going out." When he reached the doorway, he stopped and turned to look at her. "I'll be back when I think you've sobered up." Jason turned again to leave.

"If you walk out of that door, take all of your junk with you," Clara threatened him. "I'm not kidding, Mister. If you leave, don't come back!" Clara's heart froze as she hurled the words at him like daggers.

Jason stopped in his tracks at her words. He turned around and stood there staring at her with this strange look on his face. "Clara, are you kicking me out again?" he finally asked her.

Clara tried to get herself together. Why was she doing this? She didn't want Jason to leave. She wanted to stop treating Jason so badly, but she was out of control. "That's right, buster. And don't you dare come crawling back to me." There she'd said it. Now maybe she could have some peace. Maybe he'd finally leave and then she wouldn't have to spend so much time worrying that he would walk out on her one day.

Jason just stood there as if she had slapped him.

Clara prayed that he wouldn't leave. She just wanted him to tell her how much he loved her and to wrap his arms around her. Why couldn't he see that she really did love him and she didn't really want him to leave? How could a man who was so smart be so stupid?

Finally Jason sighed. "Clara, one day you're going to kick me out and I'm going to leave and not come back."

"Well, I don't care," Clara shot back at him as she stood with her fists clenched by her sides. She felt a tinge of victory at his words. She was happy that he really didn't want to go. Clara thought she'd push it a little further. Maybe she could get him to beg her to let him stay. Perhaps he'd even declare his undying love for her. "As a matter of fact, why don't you go ahead and leave and never come back. See if I care," she hissed at him.

"Fine. If that's the way you want it. Fine." Jason walked out the door.

Clara's heart sank as she watched him leave. "Wait a minute," she wanted to cry out. "You're not supposed to leave." But he had left. Clara had not expected him to go. She wanted him to tell her how she was the only woman for him and how he would die without her. But he didn't. That wasn't Jason's style. Although he had often told her of his love, he was not the begging type. He always told Clara that he wanted a woman to share his life with, one who loved him as much as he loved her. Clara did love him, but she couldn't bring herself to tell him how much. She was so afraid that if she let her guard down he would dump her. Now she had pushed him out of her life. Clara sighed as she sat down on the bed. Although she regretted her actions, this was not the first time she and Jason had fought like this. Lately, they had been fighting a lot. She didn't know what was wrong with her. Sure, her job at the Crisis

Center was getting her down, but that was nothing new. It just seemed that she had been freaking out since Jason had asked her to marry him. "Well, well, well," she thought to herself. "I've just psycho analyzed myself." Clara laughed crazily. She was freaking out because her man wanted to get married. How stupid was that? She didn't know what her problem was. She only knew that she couldn't bring herself to tell Jason that she would marry him. Then again, maybe it was her fear of being rejected. Maybe she just didn't believe that she deserved a great guy like Jason. "But why?" Clara asked herself. "Why can't I have a great guy like Jason? Why can't I have a normal life and get married and be happy?" Clara shook her head as if to clear it of the questions that were scrambling around looking for answers. "I don't need to be thinking about all of this right now." Clara looked around for her purse. "Right now, I just need to get some aspirin for this headache that won't go away," Clara said out loud as she reached for her pocketbook and searched inside for some aspirin. Anyway Jason had tricked her. They had agreed to move in together with no strings attached. Then three months after living together, he had to spoil everything by proposing to her. She still remembered that day like it was yesterday.

It was the first day of April, and Clara had just gotten in from the Center. Jason was sitting in the kitchen waiting for her like he always was when she came in.

"Hi," he said as he jumped up and came over to her. "I've been waiting for you." He kissed her on the lips. "I have a surprise for you. Why don't you go upstairs and take a shower to relax yourself?" he said turning her towards the stairs and giving her a gentle nudge. "And honey, can you put on that red dress that I love so much?"

She was a little disappointed because she had intended to just sit on the couch and watch television. But she loved Jason, and it was so cute the way he always had surprises for her. So she went up and showered and changed into the dress that he had asked her to wear. When she came down the steps, Jason whistled.

"You look absolutely gorgeous." He escorted her out to the car and drove her to their favorite restaurant. They had a lovely dinner, and as she sat looking at the dessert and coffee menu, he stood up and got down on one knee. When she looked up and saw what he was doing, she almost fainted with surprise. He took her hand in one of his, and she noticed that he had a very nice diamond ring in his other hand. The proposal was so sweet.

"Clara, I love you more than I ever imagined that I could love anyone. I realize that living with you is not enough. I want to spend the rest of my life with you as my wife. Will you marry me?"

Before she knew it, Clara sputtered out, "I-I-I can't marry you!"

Then she watched as the color drained from Jason's face. He tried to get himself together as *he got up from the floor. He put the ring back in his pocket and asked her, "What are you having for dessert?"*

"I just want to go home," Clara cried as she got up and ran out of the restaurant leaving Jason sitting there to deal with the nosy stares of the people sitting around them.

Since that day, she and Jason had a hard time getting along. It wasn't that he didn't try, but Clara felt like he had betrayed her trust in him. He knew how she felt about marriage. He knew about her parents and how they had broken up when she was ten. He knew that she didn't believe in marriage. So why did he have to go and mess up their relationship by proposing? Clara felt that she should talk to Jason, so she went downstairs to look for him. After searching the entire house, she looked outside for his car and realized that he was gone. "Oh well." She shrugged her shoulders. "I guess I'll just have another drink. He'll be back," she told herself as she went over to the bar and took out a bottle. She got a glass and sat down on the couch. Picking up the remote, she flicked on the television set. She poured herself a drink and sat back to watch television and wait for Jason.

Jennie

Clara fell asleep on the couch. When she woke up, it was morning. Her head was throbbing and she felt like crap. She looked at her watch and realized that she had only twenty minutes to get ready for work. She ran upstairs and jumped in the shower.

She arrived at the Center just in time for her first client. Her schedule that day was very busy. She saw one client after another until finally, she watched her last client walk out of her office. "What is it with these women?" she thought to herself. Everybody that came into her office that day was in the same boat. They were all either crying over how some man had done them wrong or complaining about how unfair life is. Clara was just about sick of this routine. She wondered if she should go back to school and perhaps get a degree in business management or something. Maybe she could just use her Psych degree to get a job in corporate America. In human resources or something. She'd do anything to escape the feelings of hopelessness that she felt at not being able to help the women who came to the Center.

Clara got up and walked deliberately towards the door. She needed to get to Sandra and tell her that she'd had enough for one day. She peeked outside into the waiting room. "Good," she thought. There was only one client left, and she was probably waiting to see one of the other counselors. Clara stepped out into the reception area and stood at Sandra's desk.

"Sandra, I'm heading out in a couple of minutes. Please hold all of my calls."

Sandra looked up at her with a strange expression on her face. Her eyes glanced in the direction of the woman sitting patiently in the waiting room.

"I hate to be the one to tell you this, Clara, but that one is yours."

Clara didn't believe her. She looked at the woman. She was not one of Clara's clients. There was no reason she couldn't see one of the other counselors.

"Well, I have to go," Clara said impatiently. "Let her see someone else."

Sandra smiled and said to Clara, "I would do that, but she specifically asked to see you. Clara, the woman has been waiting for over an hour."

Clara looked over at the woman who was now watching her and Sandra. "Who referred her?" she asked Sandra. "Why does she want to see me?"

Sandra shrugged her shoulders. "I don't know. She wouldn't give me much information, just her name and that she wanted to see only the counselor in that office." Sandra pointed at Clara's office as she spoke.

"Okay. What's her name?"

"Jennie," Sandra said.

"Jennie what?" Clara thought that maybe her last name would sound familiar.

"Jennie Browning." Sandra looked at Clara and raised her eyebrows. "Pretty mysterious, huh?"

Clara didn't answer her. She wondered just where this Jennie woman had come from. She wondered if she should just refuse to see her. But there was something on the inside of her that told her she had to take her. "Okay, I'll take this one," Clara said. "But no more stragglers. Okay?"

Sandra smiled at her and said, "Okay, boss lady. You got it."

"Ms. Browning." Clara called out to her mystery client. "Ms. Browning, you can come in now."

Jennie Browning got up and walked gracefully across the room. She walked with the air of a woman who knew that people were watching her. She was a beautiful woman. Her long hair framed her face just right. Clara wondered what her problem was. She looked like she didn't have a care in the world.

Clara waited for her to reach them and gestured for her to go into her office. She followed the woman into her office and closed the door. Then she walked over to her desk and sat down.

"Have a seat, Ms. Browning." Clara waved towards the couch, loveseat and armchair. She watched to see which seat the woman would take. Somehow she knew that she would choose the armchair. Jennie sat down and crossed her legs. Clara could smell her perfume as she moved. There was something different about this woman. Clara tried to figure it out, but couldn't.

"You can call me Jennie." Her voice was like silk casting a spell on all who heard it.

"Okay, Jennie." Clara jumped right in, impatient to get this over with. "How are you today?"

"Not too good, or I wouldn't be here." Jennie chuckled at her own little joke as she gazed at Clara with eyes that sparkled with mischief.

"Well, would you like to tell me why you're here today?" Although Clara felt like Jennie was playing games with her, there was something about her that Clara liked.

"Yes." Jennie smiled coyly at Clara. "I have a problem, and I really need some help." She went on, leaning towards Clara as if to tell her a secret. "You see. I'm married to this guy. Only our marriage has become really boring, and I've been seeing other men."

Clara resisted the urge to lean forward. "What do you mean when you say that you've been seeing other men? Does your husband know?"

Jennie looked at Clara intently for one moment before she replied. "Of course my husband doesn't know. Actually, one of them is a friend of his, but he only comes over when my husband's at work. I'm afraid he's getting carried away. Always telling me how much he loves me. He's started sending me flowers and cards. If he's not careful, my husband will find out about him."

Clara could imagine men falling all over them selves to be with Jennie. She knew that she was venturing out into the deep. But she had to ask.

"Are you having an affair with this man? What about the others?"

"Are you asking me if I'm having sex with these men?"

That's what Clara had asked her. Clara felt like she was being toyed with again. Jennie was playing cat and mouse with her and Clara had the strange feeling that she was the mouse. At that moment she wondered for the second time where this woman had come from. "Yes Jennie, why don't you tell me if you're having sex with these men?"

Jennie hung her head as if ashamed and responded, "Yes."

Clara had just been let in on a secret that she really didn't want to know. As she watched her new client, she could see that there was much more involved than the fact that Jennie was sleeping around on her husband. The woman sitting in the chair no longer appeared exotic and confident. She now appeared pathetic and ashamed. She had uncrossed her legs, pulled down her skirt, wrapped her arms around herself and sat cowering in the chair. Clara studied the woman for a moment.

"Jennie, may I ask you a question?"

"Yes," the woman answered in a small timid voice.

"Are you still here?"

"Yes," Jennie's voice sang sexily. "But she won't let me come out and play."

"Who won't let you come out and play?" Clara wrote split personality on her pad.

"Jennifer," Jennie answered.

"Hello Jennifer." Clara continued to write as she spoke to the shy, cowering girl.

Jennifer just sat there looking at her hands as she played with them in her lap. She nervously pulled on her fingers and then balled up her fists and pounded her two hands together.

Clara stopped writing and looked up. "Jennifer, you don't have to be afraid of me. You can talk to me. I want to help you." Clara wanted to run out of her office and get some help for this poor girl. At the same time, she wanted to go over and wrap her arms around her and tell her that everything was going to be all right. Clara felt like she knew Jennifer, but she had never seen the girl in her life. She reminded Clara of someone, but for the life of her Clara could not figure out who that someone was.

"You can't help me," Jennifer squeaked as she cowered in her chair. "She's out of control. You have no idea of the things she makes me do." She looked around as if she was looking for someone. She jumped nervously and shivered as she pulled a shabby sweater out of her bag and wrapped it around her flimsy blouse.

Clara was not sure how to proceed. She had never met anyone with a split personality before. But she was curious to find out more about the woman who had come here asking to see her. She moved a little closer to her desk and spoke softly.

"Jennifer, if you don't tell me what's going on, I can't help you," Clara said. Then she leaned back in her chair. "Jennifer. Why did you come to see me?"

Clara asked as she remembered that Jennie had wanted to see only her.

"I wanted to meet you." Jennifer spoke so softly that Clara had a hard time hearing her. "I wanted to know you better."

Clara didn't have a clue what this girl was talking about. How could she want to know her better? Clara wondered if perhaps they had met before and maybe she had somehow forgotten. "Have we met before?"

Jennifer shook her head.

"Then why me?" Clara asked again.

Jennifer looked up at her for the first time and smiled. "Because we're connected. We have a lot in common."

Clara felt strange when she heard Jennifer's answer. What could she possibly have in common with this crazy woman? Connected, she had said. That was nonsense. There was no way she could be connected to Jennie. She had never seen this woman before in her life. Clara realized that Jennie would need special handling, the type that she was not willing to provide. The only reason that she worked at the Crisis Center was to stay away from the real crazy people. This woman needed a psychiatrist. She had a split personality, and she had all of the signs of being nuts. In spite of this, Clara wanted to help her. She would refer her out to someone who was skilled in this sort of thing. She could think of a few people who she could send her to.

"Listen, Jennie or Jennifer or whoever is here right now," Clara said. "Jennifer was right. I can't help you two. Why don't I refer you to someone who can?"

"No!" Jennie was back. "We will only see you. You have to help us," she pleaded. "The geek was right. We're connected...all three of us."

Clara couldn't stop herself from shaking her head. This, she couldn't handle. She had to find a way to end this session. "Okay, why don't you let me take some information from you, and we'll see what we can do from there." She picked up her pad. "Where do you live?"

"Nope." Jennie shrugged off the sweater and sat back in the chair and crossed her legs. "We can't tell you that."

"Okay, how about your age and your occupation?"

"Thirty five and we don't work."

Clara had already figured out the last part. "Okay Jennie. How long has this been going on?"

"Well, I've been married for three years, and I have always had another man on the side." Jennie was back in full control now. It was almost as if Jennifer didn't exist.

Clara wanted to know how long this girl had been dealing with her disorder.

"Who is the oldest, Jennie, you or Jennifer?"

"You silly counselor you."

Clara sensed that Jennie was still playing games with her.

"I already told you. We're both 35. I've known the geek all of my life."

Clara twirled her pencil around and around. "Right," she said. "How silly of me." Two could play this game. "Okay ladies. Time's up. Here." She stood to her feet and reached for Jennie's chart. "Take this to my secretary and she'll schedule you for your next appointment. When you come back, I want to see pictures of your childhood. Okay?" When all else failed, Clara always went the childhood route. Most of the problems that she encountered here at the Center started when her clients were kids.

"Okay," Jennie answered as she took the sheet of paper and sashayed out of the office leaving the sweet smell of her expensive perfume behind her.

Clara stood there for a moment. Then she sat back down and put her head in her hands. "Just what I need. A real psycho," she said as she straightened up in her chair and reached over to turn on her Dictaphone machine. Taking a deep breath, she started recording her notes about Jennie and Jennifer. She wondered why they had come in to see her specifically. She could only remember the words that both of them had spoken.

"We're connected. All three of us," they had both said.

Clara wondered again how in the world they could be connected. After all, she didn't know Jennie or Jennifer or whatever her name was. She had never laid eyes on the woman before today. She couldn't help but feel a little eerie about this whole situation. "Boy," she thought. "There are some weird people in this world and I have to be the one trying to help everybody keep it together. I need a drink." Clara got up and locked the door. Then she reached into her bag and took out a bottle of booze. She sat back and took a long swig right from the bottle. As the warm liquid flooded her insides, Clara started to feel a little better. Just as she turned the bottle up for another swallow, there was a knock on the door. She stuffed the bottle back into her bag. Then she jumped up and opened the door. Sandra was standing there. She looked at Clara with her head tilted slightly to the side and a strange look on her face.

"Are you okay?" she asked.

"Yes." Clara walked back to her desk to escape Sandra's scrutiny. She ran her hand over her hair and straightened her skirt. "Why?" Clara sat in her chair and picked up a pack of mints.

"Well, that lady seemed a little strange and you usually come right out after you've had a weirdo."

"You can say that again." Clara popped a mint into her mouth. "That one was strange." She scratched her head as she recalled her recent encounter with Jennie. "Can you believe she has a split personality?"

"Split personality?" Sandra opened her eyes wide in disbelief. "Are you serious?"

"Un-huh." Clara picked up Jennie's chart from her desk. "I'm very serious. She said the strangest thing to me." Clara stared at the chart without really seeing it.

"What's that?"

"When I asked her why she had wanted to see me, she said it's because we're connected." Clara was still staring at the chart.

Sandra looked at her boss. "Connected? Do you know her or did someone refer her to you?"

Clara put the chart down on her desk. She hadn't thought about that. "Oh, maybe that's it. Maybe she knows someone in my family or something." Clara felt a little less scared. "I was so freaked out by her split personality that I forgot to ask her if someone had referred her to me." Clara laughed. "I need a vacation. I'll bet that's it." Clara and Sandra both laughed at the odd turn of events. But Clara still could not relax. This was all too weird for her. She wished that she knew what had really led Jennie to the Center.

"Well, I hope she does know somebody that I know. Either way, this day was just too weird for me. I probably need to refer her out."

"You're probably right." Sandra laughed. "And remember, the lady has a split personality. She needs more help than we can give her here."

"You can say that again," Clara said. "Why don't you work on a referral for her? You can put it in her file for the next time she comes in."

Sandra had picked up a pad from Clara's desk and was already making a note of Clara's instructions.

"I've got to get out of here." Clara picked up her bag and headed for the door. "I'll see you tomorrow." she said as she passed Sandra. "Lock up for me, okay?"

Sandra nodded although Clara had already left the room.

The Phone Call

Twenty minutes later, Clara pulled into her driveway. She was happy to be home at last. But she was disappointed when she didn't see Jason's car in the driveway. As she put her key in the lock, she heard the phone ringing. She dropped her bags on the kitchen floor and reached for the phone hoping it was Jason.

"Hello," she shouted into the receiver, out of breath.

"Hello Clara."

Clara was surprised to hear her friend's voice. "Hi Francine. What's happening, girl? It's great to hear your voice!"

"Same here, girl," Francine said. "What's going on?"

Clara grabbed a kitchen chair and sat down. "Nothing much. I just got in from the Center. How have you been? I haven't heard from you in months."

"Well, the phone does work both ways. Have you broken your fingers?"

Clara had suspected that Francine would say something like that. That is exactly the reason she hadn't called her over the past few months.

"No, my fingers aren't broken." Clara was not going to fight with Francine. "I've just been so busy at the Center."

"Oh, I see you're still hanging out with those crazy people." Francine laughed loudly.

Clara laughed along with her. Her laughter echoed in the quiet house. "Well, I feel like I'm in good company. After all, we're all crazy in our own way. Besides, I don't feel so bad about my issues after talking to my clients at the Center."

"Well, you have a good point there." Francine's voice became serious. "Maybe I should become a counselor. Do you think that would help me?"

Clara took a deep breath. "Oh boy," she thought. "Here it comes."

"Do you know what these people are doing now?" Francine's voice got louder.

"No. But I have a feeling you're going to tell me." Only Clara really didn't want to hear it.

Francine went on as if she had not heard Clara. "They're all ganging up on me because I'm still not talking to my mother."

Clara didn't agree with Francine's behavior. The girl had been at war with her mother for years. "Well, you know how I feel about that." Clara knew that Francine was looking for someone to take her side on this issue. However, Clara could not compromise how she felt about the way her friend treated her mother.

"Yeah, yeah. I know how you feel, and you know how I feel." Francine spoke in such a harsh tone that Clara just wanted to get off the phone. "I will never forgive that woman for the way she's treated me all these years. Never! First, she made me take care of all of her babies. Then I had to work like a dog around the house, and she had the nerve to call me names like slut and whore anytime a boy wanted to take me out."

Clara sighed.

"Does that sigh mean you don't want to hear this?"

"No Francine. It means that I really wish that you could put the past behind you. You're forty years old now. How long are you going to hold this grudge against your mother?"

"Clara, of all the people that I can talk to about this, you're the only one that really understands how I feel. Don't tell me you're turning against me too."

"I'm not turning against you and I'm definitely not taking sides on this issue." Clara thought carefully about her next words. "It's just that you only get one mother in this life. For God's sake, you can't just stop talking to your mother."

"So you're telling me that no matter how badly she treats me, I'm supposed to just ignore it and act like it's not happening?" Francine's voice was as cold as ice.

"No, that's not what I'm saying. I'm simply telling you that you need to try to forgive your mother and find a way to get along with her." Clara paused before she added. "She won't be here forever, you know."

Francine was very quiet on the other end of the phone.

"Francine, are you still there?"

Francine sniffled and Clara knew that she was crying again. This was their normal routine, Francine would rant and rave about how much she hated her mother and then she would start crying when Clara didn't take her side. Clara felt bad for the girl. She wished she could help her but she was having a tough time right now herself. Who was going to help her to deal with her own problems? Clara knew she couldn't let Francine hang up like this.

"Listen Francine, I didn't mean to come down on you so hard. It's just that I want you to be happy, and I know that this whole situation is making you miserable. Don't you know that bitterness and resentment will eat away at you and you'll have all types of health problems if you keep going like this?"

"I know *Dr. Clara* and it's too late. I'm already having problems. Emotional problems. And it's all her fault. I hate her."

"You don't hate her." Clara tried to calm Francine down. "You're just really mad at her right now. Like I said, I think you should talk to her. Why don't you take her out to lunch?"

"No, that's quite alright." Francine's voice was sad now. "You don't know what she did to me. You didn't have to grow up being treated like crap." She sounded like she was going to cry again.

A flame of anger lapped at Clara's heart. She wanted to tell her friend off. How dare she call her house and play the victim. Clara hated it when people assumed that her life had been one big party. But she didn't dare get into that with Francine. Besides, her life was nobody's business.

"Listen." She tried to keep her voice calm. "I know that it may not seem like it, but you'll get through this. I understand what you're going through and I know it's hard for you to deal with."

"Yeah, it's tough. I just want to stay away from them all for a little while. I want them to stop calling me and trying to make me feel guilty." She let out a big sigh. "You know Clara, I said that I hate my mother, and the sad part about it is I think I really do. I'm so mad at her for the way my life turned out."

"I understand all of that." Clara carefully chose her next words. "Francine, you can't control what happened in your past, but you can go forward and take control of your future. You can choose to be happy and your life can be different."

"How can I be happy? When my whole family is against me."

Clara knew that she was not getting through to Francine. "Listen Francine. Just think about what I've said. Even if you have to stay away from your entire family long enough to get some happiness back into your life, then do it." Clara wished she could find a way to help her friend. "No one deserves to be this unhappy. Francine, you need to choose to be happy no matter who gets upset. Okay?"

"Listen, I have to go." Francine seemed to be in a hurry all of a sudden. "Thanks for taking the time to talk to me. I just needed to get this off of my chest. I'm still angry, but I feel a little better. Thanks Clara."

"No problem. Call me if you need me. Day or night."

"Okay. Bye."

"Bye." Clara reached over to put the phone back into the charger. "Whew," she sighed. "What next?" she asked out loud as she picked up her stuff and headed up the stairs.

Heartbreak

Clara jumped when she walked into her bedroom and saw Jason sitting there. He must have come in while she was on the phone. Clara thought it was strange that she hadn't heard him when he came in. Perhaps he was here the whole time. But then, where was his car? Anyway, Clara's heartbeat quickened as she looked at her man. She loved him but they definitely needed to talk.

"Hi." Clara's voice was as cold as ice. Although she was happy that he was home, she couldn't help being angry. Jason hadn't come home last night. As far as Clara was concerned, he had walked out on her and didn't even bother to call to say that he would be out all night. She vaguely remembered their fight from last night. She wondered if she had kicked him out again. That sure would explain why he had stayed out all night. Jason looked like he had a lot on his mind as he sat down on the edge of the bed.

"Hi Clara." He had a distant look on his face. Clara got a nervous twinge in the pit of her stomach. She had never seen that haunted look on her man's face before.

"Where have you been?" she asked him, suddenly feeling like she didn't want to know.

"I had to get away for a little while." Jason sat there still staring off into space. "Just to clear my head."

"What's the deal?" Clara stood in front of him. "You know we agreed that we wouldn't stay out all night. Why didn't you call?"

Jason shook his head. "Listen, Clara. You're the one who came in here drunk last night and jumped all over me for nothing. You pushed me away just like you've been doing for the past couple of months." He lifted his head to look up at her, his eyes meeting hers for the first time since they had started talking.

Clara trembled at the look in his eyes. She was pierced to the core by the pain and the anguish that she saw reflected in the windows of his soul. She started to speak, but Jason held up his hand to stop her.

"No. Tonight you're going to let me talk for a change. I don't appreciate the way you've been acting." He stood up and shoved his hands into his pockets. "I don't know if you realize it, but you've been treating me like a dog lately. No. Worse."

Clara tried to object, but Jason stopped her again, this time holding up both hands in front of him. "No. I said I'm talking tonight. You're always yelling at me and cursing me out like you can't stand me or something. When we first got together, you treated me like a king. You respected me and you never raised your voice at me." Jason's eyes filled with unshed tears. "I asked you to marry me, and you shot me down." Now his eyes flashed with anger. "You embarrassed me in front of a whole restaurant full of people. I couldn't have been more ashamed if you had slapped me in the face." He stopped talking and took a deep breath "Okay. I understand that you don't want to get married. I should've realized that you really meant it when you first told me that you never wanted to." He stopped again and ran his hand over his hair. "But I don't understand why you've been acting so weird around here lately. You've been disappearing and coming in late almost every day."

Clara looked at him and realized that he was waiting for an answer. "Jason, I'm sorry. I don't know what's wrong with me lately. I..."

"I think your job is too much for you," Jason cut in. "Our problems really got worse when you started working at that place."

Clara knew what was coming next. She really didn't want to go through this again. She looked around the room for a way out. If only she could stop this conversation and find a way to make things okay again. Things were way out of control and Clara's heart filled with a sense of dread. Things could only get worse now. Jason had never acted this way before. Clara was scared.

Jason reached out and grabbed her by the arms "Clara, I think you need to get out of that place. It's doing something weird to you. Baby, you've changed."

Clara couldn't believe that Jason was pleading with her to quit her job again. She hated it when he did this to her. Once again he was trying to make her choose him over her job. She couldn't do that. She couldn't leave the Center. The Center was her reason for living. She had to help those women.

"Jason, I don't think it's fair for you to blame our problems on my job at the Center." She moved away from him. Suddenly exhausted, she sat down on the bed. "I know I often come home worn out from hearing all about other women's problems. And I must admit to you, sometimes I do feel like quitting. But I can't. In some strange way, I'm connected to these women." The words echoed in her head after she said them. "What was this connected stuff? Oh well, it sounded good anyway," she thought as she looked down at the shoes that she had left on the floor this morning. "What a mess," she thought as she looked around the room and pushed away a suit and some blouses that she had thrown on the bed.

"That's exactly what I'm saying, baby. You're connected to them, and you have disconnected yourself from me and my love." He rubbed his eyes.

Clara noticed that he looked very tired, as if he had been up all night.

"I can't take being second fiddle to the Center and your crazy clients anymore."

Clara had heard this before. She was tired of fighting with Jason. How could she tell him that these women were not crazy? That they were just like her - confused, abused and disillusioned about life? At that moment, she didn't want to talk anymore.

She just wanted him to hold her. She reached out to him and pulled him over to sit with her on the bed. "Listen Jason, why don't we just lay down? We can hold each other and continue talking." Clara spoke softly in his ear as she put her arms around him.

Jason jumped up and moved away from her. "No Clara. That won't work tonight. I can't just be your lover. I need to be a priority in your life. I know that you're not used to men wanting to make a commitment. But I want a wife. And I want kids."

Clara's eyes got big when Jason mentioned kids. That was one of the reasons she wouldn't marry him. She never wanted to have kids. But Jason didn't know that and she couldn't find the words to tell him. "Jason, give me some time to get myself together. Let me think about all of this."

"Okay Clara." Jason nodded his head as if that had been the answer he was waiting for. "As a matter of fact, that's exactly what I had in mind."

Clara let out a sigh of relief. "Great." She stood up and straightened her skirt. "Baby, let's go out tonight. We can go downtown and have some drinks and listen to some Karaoke, and then we can come back home and make love."

"No. That's not a good idea. Clara, you need to get yourself together and see what you really want out of life."

"Yeah, I agree with that." Clara's laugh was a nervous one. "In the meantime, let's just have fun like we used to." She rubbed his chest. "Come on. Let's make up for last night."

Jason angrily removed her hands. "Stop it, Clara!" He seemed flustered.

Alarmed by his reaction, Clara backed away from Jason. She had never seen him act like this before. He had never turned down making love to her. All of a sudden Clara felt like something was dreadfully wrong.

"Don't you even care where I was last night?" he yelled at her.

"No. Don't tell me," Clara thought. Somehow she knew that she was not going to like what was coming next.

"I left here and I was so mad at you. I met this woman and she said all of the right things. It was like she knew me."

Clara looked at him as though she was seeing him for the first time. "What did he just say?" she asked herself, "What did he mean by he met this woman? And what is all of this crap about her saying all of the right things?" Clara felt like she was in the twilight zone. This could not be happening to her. "Are you telling me that you were with another woman?" she asked him slowly and deliberately. She just wished that somebody would stop the world right now so that she could get off. "Ouch," Clara thought as she reached for her chest on the left side. What was that pain in her chest?

"Yes." Jason's voice was barely audible. His lips were moving, but Clara refused to believe that he was saying the words that were going like a knife through her heart. "But it was innocent. Nothing happened.

We just talked and laughed all night just like you and I used to do."

"All night?" The words echoed in Clara's head. She felt like her heart was being ripped out of her chest. "You bastard!" She couldn't stop the tears from flowing down her face as she yelled at him. "You come in here trying to make me feel bad because I won't marry you, and you've been out all night with some woman!" Clara couldn't begin to measure the level of betrayal that she felt at this moment. "That's exactly why I wouldn't marry you," she hissed like the meanest of snakes. "You're just like all the other men out there. You're nothing but a lying, cheating dog!"

"Clara, that's not fair."

"It is fair, and it's the truth!" Her voice got louder and she began to feel hysterical. "At the first sign of trouble, you go out and shack up with some whore!" Clara was furious. "Thank you for helping me to make up my mind." Clara's world was crumbling into little pieces. "I don't need this crap. I have enough problems."

"What problems, Clara?"

"None of your business!!" Her words slammed into him. "My problems are my problems and they're nobody's business! Not yours. Not nobody's!"

Jason shrugged his shoulders in defeat and tilted his head. "Clara, that's what you've been telling me since we've been together." He looked into her eyes as if he was trying to see inside of her. "You know what?" He went on without waiting for her to answer. "I finally believe you."

Clara felt like she was in quicksand. She was sinking, and she couldn't find anything to hold on to. "Just go!" she shouted. "I know that you're going anyway, so just go on back to your whore."

Jason headed for the door.

"No," Clara stopped him. "Take your stuff." Clara was beyond stopping now. "All of it."

"Are you kicking me out?"

"No." Clara had finally stopped crying. "I'm asking you to leave. We both know that it's over. This other woman has given you what I can't anymore."

"But you can if you want to." Jason reached for her.

"No, Jason. I can't." Clara stood frozen in his arms. "I've lost my trust in you. You've hurt me, and I don't think I can ever trust you again." She steeled her heart against the tears that threatened to overwhelm her again.

Jason tried to reason with her. "Clara, you know that I love you."

"No, you don't love me. If you did, you wouldn't have been with another woman last night." Clara looked at him with murderous eyes. "Now get out."

He moved away from her and headed towards the door. "Okay Clara, I'll go. I'll be back for my things tomorrow while you're at work."

Clara nodded. Her heart cried for her to beg him to stay. But she couldn't. He had committed the ultimate betrayal. Another woman? There was no forgiveness for that. How could he be with another woman?" Clara watched him as he stopped and turned to look at her. He was so handsome. That was

54

one of the things that had always scared her about him. Why would someone like him want to be with someone like her? It didn't matter now anyway. He had let her down just like she always knew he would. All men were like that. They hung around with you just long enough to get their fill, until the next pretty face or nice figure came along, and then they cheated on you or dumped you or both. But Clara wasn't having any of that. She'd dumped him before he even had a chance to dump her.

Jason was still standing there looking at Clara as if waiting for her to tell him to stay. Finally, he sighed and started for the door again. When he reached the door, he stopped and turned around.

At that moment Clara wished that he would beg her to let him stay. She watched him carefully to see what he would say.

"I'll leave the keys on the table tomorrow."

That wasn't what he was supposed to say. Clara nodded again. Her heart was pounding. She didn't want him to leave. But she knew he had to go.

Jason took one more look at the woman he loved and left.

Clara sat on the edge of the bed. She felt numb all over. She couldn't believe that Jason had the nerve to tell her that he had spent the night with another woman. How dare he violate her trust like that? She would have preferred not to know where he'd been. Who was this woman anyway? How could this man who she'd shared so much with even think about being with another woman? Clara looked around at the bedroom where they had shared so much love over the past four months. They had spent many precious moments in this room. Clara remembered the day when they decided to live together.

They had been dating for two years and Jason asked her if she wanted to think about getting a little more serious.

"Serious?" she questioned him. "Don't we spend all of our free time together? I really don't see how we can be any more serious without being married."

Jason looked at her with a quizzical expression on his face. "Baby, that's exactly what I'm talking about. You don't seem to want any kind of commitment from me."

"Yes I do," she assured him as she moved closer to him. "I want to know that you'll always be there for me. I want to know that I can trust you and that you'll never betray me."

Jason took her right hand and brought the palm to his lips. "Baby, I'll never betray you. My heart belongs to you and you only."

Clara smiled at him and moved to sit on his lap. "Good," she purred. "That's all I need."

"Clara." Jason refused to let her off that easy. "I was thinking that maybe we could move in together. I mean, especially since we practically live together anyway."

Clara studied his face to see if he was serious. Finally, after a minute she told him, "Okay, big boy. We'll get a place together. Only, don't try any funny business."

"No funny business," Jason promised with a big smile on his face as he leaned over to kiss Clara passionately on the lips.

"Well." Clara spoke her thoughts out loud, "That was the first promise that he broke on the night that he proposed. And now I find out that he's betrayed me by spending the night with another woman." Clara sat back against the headboard and folded her arms. She had been such a fool. She thought Jason was so special, but he had lied to her, and now her heart was broken. Clara wept uncontrollably. She cried for the love she'd just lost. She cried for the broken promises, and she cried simply because the tears refused to stop.

Sunday Dinner

Two days later, Clara sat at the table and looked around the kitchen. She hadn't been to her mother's house in at least a month. She wouldn't have come today if her mother had not begged her to come and see her. So, in spite of her not wanting to come, here she was and she was already ready to go home. Clara tried to think of an excuse to leave early. She wanted to get out of there before her sister came. She and her sister just didn't get along. Clara loved her sister, but her sister seemed to resent her. No matter how hard she tried Clara just couldn't get along with her sister. Clara wished that things could be like they used to be when they were kids. Her sister had always looked after her and taken care of her. Things had changed after her father moved out.

"Clara honey, you're not eating." Her mother always watched to make sure that everyone ate huge servings of the food she prepared.

"Mom, I'm not really hungry." Clara pushed the food around on her plate. "Besides, I'm trying to lose weight."

"You might as well accept the size that you are. Once you get to be a certain age, the weight stays."

"Well Mom, you may be right but I can at least try to look good." Clara pushed the plate away from her. "I always feel better when I'm fit."

Just then her older sister came into the kitchen. Clara braced herself and stood up to hug Loretta.

"Oh, hi Sis." Loretta half hugged Clara back and walked over to the stove.

"Hi Loretta, how are you?" Clara forced her voice not to give away the hurt she felt as she stood there watching her big sister.

"Oh the same old stuff. Hi Mom, what's for dinner?" Loretta asked as one by one she lifted the lid of each pot and peeked inside.

"Hi Mom. What's for dinner? You come in here and you don't even give me a hug and all you want to know is what's for dinner." Her tone was so harsh that it cut through the air like a sharp blade.

Clara and Loretta both turned to look at their mother. Although Clara had heard her mother use this tone of voice with her sister before, she never understood why. And it always made her angry. Her mother treated her sister like a stepchild, and she knew that her relationship with her sister was strained partly because of the way their mother treated Loretta. Clara hated the way her mother treated her sister but she didn't want to cause trouble so she had become very good at hiding her feelings of resentment towards her mother. She was glad that her mother's attention was focused elsewhere as she walked back to her chair and tried to calm down.

"Aw, Ma. What did I do this time?" Loretta whined with a hint of impatience. "Every time I come over here you pick on me."

"That's because you need to get yourself together. Look at you." Her mother had a look of pure disgust on her face. "You didn't even comb your hair today."

Clara cringed as her mother continued to attack Loretta. She tried hard to think of a good reason to get out of there.

"That's because I like the natural look. What do you want Mom? For me to be perfect like your precious little Clara?"

Clara stiffened in her chair. She hated coming here. Every time she came, Loretta and her mother had the same argument. Then Loretta would go and find something to drink and end up drunk. After that, things would really heat up. She vowed to herself that she would leave before they got that far tonight.

"Come on Loretta, that's not necessary." Clara's voice cracked with emotion.

"Oh, that's easy for you to say. You've always been the favorite around here. You and Daddy Dearest." She spun around and faced her mother. "Our mother has always hated me. Isn't that right Mom?"

"I don't hate you. I just wish that you could be more like your sister."

"See. What did I tell you? More like your sister. More like your sister. I wish you could be more like your sister," Loretta taunted as she put her face into Clara's. "She thinks you're perfect. You've always been such a goody-two shoes. You make me sick." Loretta turned around and headed for the counter. She picked up a bottle of brandy and poured some into a glass.

"That's your problem now." Her mother was not finished with Loretta. "You need to leave that stuff alone. That stuff has you all messed up."

"Well, look who's talking." Loretta stood glaring at her mother. "You've been drunk every single day of my life. And now you want to stand here and preach to me."

"I can handle my liquor." Her mother defended herself.

"Well, I can handle my liquor too." Loretta swallowed the liquid from the glass. "Ahhhh. That's good stuff." She tilted the bottle and poured another drink.

Her mother shook her head and sighed.

Clara sat and watched the two of them. She had seen this scene played out many times before. As a matter of fact, they went through this each and every time she came to her mother's house. Clara watched as her mother moved over to the counter and picked up the bottle. Then as if in a daze, she also got up and walked over to pour herself a drink.

The three of them stood there in the kitchen, looking at each other. Clara wondered what her mother and Loretta were thinking as they stood there glaring at each other. She wondered what drove them to drink all the time. She thought for a moment about why she had started drinking so much lately. Finally, Clara finished her drink and put her glass down on the counter next to the almost empty bottle. "Mom, thanks for the dinner. I have to get up early so I'm going to leave now." For a moment, Clara thought she saw a panicked expression cross her mother's face.

"Why do you have to leave so early?"

"She probably wants to get home to her man." Loretta leaned against the counter nursing her drink.

"Yeah. Why didn't Jason come over today? He loves my cooking."

"Jason is history." Clara almost enjoyed the look of surprise on her sister's face. "Jason is like every other man that I've ever loved."

"Oh, Clara. I'm sorry." Her mother picked up the bottle and poured herself another drink. Then she walked over to the kitchen table and plopped down into a chair.

Clara looked at her mother. Her mother was only 55 and she was single. She had never remarried after she and Clara's father split. Clara always wondered why a beautiful woman like her mother chose to be alone. She wondered if she would end up like her. "Mom, it's okay. I'll be fine. Besides, only the strong survive. Right?" Clara reminded her mother of this lesson that she had taught her throughout her childhood, whenever she started to cry out for her father, or whenever she was disappointed or worried about something.

"Yes that is true," her mother replied as she finished off her drink. "Only the strong survive."

Loretta's laughter interrupted their conversation. "That's a joke. None of us are surviving and we're sure not strong. We're just weak and lonely women. The saddest part about it is that we will probably die that way." She shook her head in disgust. "This family is all messed up." She pointed at Clara. "Your precious father messed this whole family up." She turned and stared coldly at their mother. "And you let him." She poured another drink and left the room, but not before a final stab at Clara and her mother. "This sure is a messed up family. I hate being in this family."

Clara looked at her mother. Her mother looked really sad as she sat hanging her head at the kitchen table. Clara wanted to go over and comfort her, but she didn't know how. She hardly ever saw her mother like this. The woman was a matriarch. She was a strong woman, and she always displayed that strength to her children. But Clara saw a different woman sitting there. She looked tired. And she looked like she was worried about something.

"Mom?" Clara walked over and peered down at her mother. "Mom, is everything okay?"

Her mother looked up at her and a surge of fear shot through Clara.

"Clara, your mother is tired. I'm tired of fighting with your sister, and I'm tired of trying to make up for the past. It's been twenty-five years since I put your father out, and that girl still won't let it die. She hates your father and she hates me."

Clara didn't know what to say. She just wanted to get out of there. She could see that her mother wanted to talk this out, but she couldn't bear to stay and listen.

"Mom, I have to go." She bent down and hugged her mother. "I love you. Remember, only the strong survive, and you are the strongest woman that I know."

Her mother smiled at her. But somehow the smile didn't look sincere. "Don't worry baby. Your old mother is going to be okay. Now that's a promise."

"Another promise," Clara thought as she walked out of the kitchen. "Another promise to be broken, just like my heart." She walked out of the house and immediately started to feel better. Safely in her car, she looked over at her mother's house. There was just something about being in that house with her family that she hated. She loved her mother, but she hated coming to that house. She always dreaded coming there, and she always left with a heavy heart. Her mother had kicked her father out twenty-five years ago, but the entire family knew that she still loved him. She even talked of getting back together with him one day. Clara never understood their relationship. She never understood why her mother would want to go back to a man like her father. When they were together, all they did was drink and fight. Then they would make up and drink and fight some more. Who would want to go back to something like that?

Clara turned the key in the ignition and pulled out into the traffic. She shook herself to get rid of the ugly feeling that was wrapped around her. She turned on the radio and tried to clear her head of all of this family drama. Her sister was right. This family was all messed up.

Lauren

Clara sat in her office across from the girl who was sitting on the edge of the loveseat. Lauren was a pretty girl. She had curly brown hair and big brown eyes. She wore very little makeup, and there was something wholesome and innocent about her. Clara always liked spending time with Lauren.

Lauren was having problems with her long-term boyfriend Tony. Tony had dumped Lauren for the third time last month because he said he was tired of her daughter acting like a spoiled brat and getting away with it. A week later, he had started hanging out with one of his old girlfriends. Lauren had come into Clara's office swearing that she would never take him back again.

Clara was pretty confident that Lauren wouldn't go back to him this time. She'd already taken this man back two times, once when he left her because his ex-wife had begged him to come back to her and again when he ran off with an old girlfriend that he bumped into at a friend's party. The same party that he had decided not to take Lauren to. He had disappeared with this girl for three weeks before crawling back to Lauren, begging for forgiveness.

Lauren sat there practically glowing.

Although Clara was happy to see her in such a good mood, she wondered what was going on with Lauren. "So...how are things going with you and your daughter?"

"Oh. Okay. She can still be a little stubborn sometimes. But, the best thing that's happened is Tony and I have been talking and we've started hanging out together."

Clara couldn't believe her ears. Why in the world would Lauren want to take Tony back? This man had broken her heart not once, not twice, but three times.

"Tell me Lauren, why did you take him back?"

The girl blushed as she fidgeted in her seat. "Well, I wouldn't say that we're back together. We're just friends."

"What does that mean?"

"Well, it's just like when we were in the beginning of our relationship. We hang out together. We go dancing. To the movies. You know. Stuff." Lauren sat back and crossed her legs.

"Are you two intimate?"

Lauren's grin was a dead giveaway. "Well, I wouldn't say that we're intimate like we used to be. We just enjoy being together, and as long as we're not in a relationship, there's no pressure."

"No pressure for who?" Clara asked as she fought to keep from yelling. She wondered how Lauren could be so naïve? "Whose idea was this friendship anyway?" she asked.

"It kind of just happened. Tony kept calling me and coming by. And then there were the flowers." Lauren's eyes twinkled as she gestured towards the flowers on Clara's desk. "He kept sending me flowers and these really sweet notes."

Clara looked at the flowers that had arrived that morning and remembered the note that Jason had sent with them asking her to call him. She had been too busy to even think about calling him or what she would say if she did. She was still in so much pain. But, she did miss him terribly.

"Tony calls me every day just to say hello." Lauren was beaming as she continued.

"Could it be that you enjoy the thrill of having Tony pursue you?"

"Yeah, I guess you could say that. Clara, he's so sweet."

"I guess he's treating you really nice right now."

"Yeah, really nice."

"Well, what about your daughter?"

Lauren flinched as if Clara had sprinkled cold water on her. "What?"

"You know. Your daughter. The one that Tony can't seem to get along with. What about her?"

Lauren blinked and rubbed her hands together. "Oh, she's afraid that I'm going to get back with Tony. She says that she doesn't want me to." Lauren rested her hands on her lap. "She doesn't like the fact that he keeps hurting me every time he leaves."

Clara nodded her head. Now maybe they could get somewhere. "Okay. So since you and Tony are only friends, is he getting along better with your daughter?"

"No. Not really. We haven't really all spent that much time together. But when we do, she's pretty sad."

"Have you and Tony had any fights since you've been friends again?"

Lauren looked sad. "Yeah. He says I need to make up my mind about us soon. He says he's not going to wait forever for me."

"And what was your response to that?"

"I told him that I wouldn't let him pressure me into getting back together with him. I told him that if he really loved me he would wait."

Clara watched Lauren's eyes. "And what did he have to say about that?"

Lauren looked down at her hands and then up at Clara again. "He told me that he has to go on with his life. He said if I really loved him, I would take him back."

Clara twirled her pencil around and around as she thought about this situation. "Lauren, tell me one reason you'd want to take him back."

Lauren rolled her eyes up towards the ceiling and back down again as if searching for a good reason to take Tony back. "I guess because I love him."

Clara sat back in her chair, still playing with her pencil. "And another?"

Lauren squinted her eyes, then opened them and replied slowly, "Because I feel so good when we're together."

Clara sat forward again. "Okay, Lauren. What about the times that you feel bad? What about the fights? What about your daughter?"

"I don't know about all of that. I only know that I love him." She paused and thought about her next words. "And Clara, I need him. I don't know what my life would be like without him. I mean what if I decided not to take him back and I wake up one morning and realize that I made the biggest mistake of my life?" Her eyes locked into Clara's. "What would I do then?"

On the one hand, Clara wanted to shake this woman. But on the other, she understood exactly what she meant. "I know what you mean, Lauren. But if you lost this man, I think that you would survive. Don't you?"

Lauren shook her head no. "No, I don't think that I would. I really don't think that I would."

Clara sat there wondering why a pretty woman like Lauren would put up with someone like Tony. She could never figure out why women put so much of themselves into their relationships. Tony was obviously bad news, but Lauren was willing to give him another chance. Clara wondered what it felt like to love someone so much that you would put that person's needs and wants in front of your own and, in Lauren's case, in front of your own daughter's. Clara looked over at the woman sitting before her and noticed that she was also deep in thought.

"Okay Lauren."

Lauren turned her eyes toward Clara.

"Listen Lauren. We have some work to do. If you think that you can't live without this man who keeps hurting you, we need to take our next visit to find out why."

Lauren nodded in agreement.

"Now, please don't do anything crazy before you come back to see me."

Lauren nodded again.

"Stay friends with him if you must. But please don't take it any further."

Lauren was staring straight ahead as if in a trance, still nodding her head.

Clara was concerned because Lauren didn't seem to be listening to her.

"Lauren I'm serious." Clara wanted to stress the need for Lauren to take it slow. "You have been hurt so much in this relationship." Clara watched Lauren closely. "I want you to tell Tony that you need some time to heal and that you want to take it slow. Okay?"

"Okay," Lauren agreed almost before Clara had finished speaking.

Because of her quick response Clara didn't believe that she meant it but there was not much more she could do. Clara decided to put an end to their session. "Okay, why don't you stop out front and make an appointment to see me in a couple of weeks?" Clara said as she stood to her feet.

"Okay." Lauren smiled as she got up. "Don't worry. I'll be fine." She reached over and picked up her purse from the table. "The worst and the best that I can do is follow my heart."

71

Clara fought back the words that were trying to push past her teeth. That was the problem now. Lauren was too busy following her heart to see that this guy was no good for her. Clara watched Lauren waltz out the door. Clara shook her head. "Why do I even bother?" she asked herself. She stared at the roses on her desk "These flowers are so beautiful." Clara reached out to touch a rose petal. "Why can't life be like this, smooth and sweet?"

Lauren had said she would follow her heart. Follow her heart? Clara looked at the phone and wondered what it felt like to just follow your heart. She thought about calling Jason but her heart was beating too fast. "Follow your heart...follow your heart." The words danced in Clara's head. "The worst I can do is follow my heart."

The Dinner

Lauren was worried that if she didn't take Tony back it could be the biggest mistake of her life. As she sat looking at the phone, Clara thought about what the girl had said. She got up and closed the door to her office. Then she walked back to her desk and eased herself down into her chair. "What a life," Clara thought as she reached out and touched the beautiful roses again. Jason knew she loved roses. He had also sent roses last week, with another note asking her to call him. She'd thrown the flowers and the note away, determined that she would never talk to him again. He had cheated on her, and even if he didn't, it hurt too much to think about him spending the night with another woman.

Clara opened her desk drawer and took out the note that came with the flowers today.

She read the note again for the tenth time. Jason had written, *"I love you. Please call me so that we can talk. I miss you. Jason."*

Before she could stop herself, she picked up the phone and dialed the number to his office.

"Hello. Jason Conway speaking."

"Hi." Clara's voice was raspy because of the lump in her throat.

"Clara? Hi Clara. I'm so glad you called."

"Look Jason...I...I just wanted to thank you for the flowers."

"Oh, you mean you didn't call to say you miss me?"

Clara heard the laughter in his voice.

When she didn't answer, Jason asked, "Don't you miss me, Clara?"

Again Clara didn't answer.

"Listen Clara. I was just going over to Romeo's to get something to eat. Do you think you could meet me there?"

Clara hesitated. "I...I don't know if I'm ready to see you Jason."

"Clara, it's only a spaghetti dinner. Why don't I pick you up?"

"No!"

"Clara, we have to talk." Something in his voice told Clara that she needed to go and at least talk to Jason about what had happened.

"You're right. We do need to talk."

"Good. I'll pick you up in half an hour."

"No. I have to drive myself. I'll meet you there- say- in about thirty minutes."

"Thirty minutes. I'll see you there, Clara."

"Okay Bye."

"Bye for now Clara."

Clara sat holding the phone. She couldn't believe that she'd agreed to meet Jason. How was she going to face him after she'd thrown him out of her life? She tried to think of a way out of going. She took a mirror out of her bag and studied her face. She looked good. In spite of the mess that her life was in, she still managed to look pretty good. Jason always told her that she was beautiful. She didn't think so. She just thought that she was okay looking, maybe even cute, but nothing spectacular.

She was glad that she had on her blue suit today. It was Jason's favorite. He liked it when she wore suits. He once told her that she should have been on Wall Street instead of some second-rate women's crisis center. They spent so much time fighting about her job. He hated it from the day she first started. She loved it from day one. Although she got sick of hearing the same old problems, she somehow felt that she was important to these women. Most of them really depended on her to listen to them and give them sensible solutions to their problems. Not that her advice changed anything, but Clara had to keep trying.

She stood up and reached for her purse and keys. Standing in the middle of the floor, she looked around the office. When she was in this place she felt good about herself. Here in this crisis center where women came to bare their souls to her, she felt that her life was worth something. While she was here, she felt that she was somebody. She didn't know what she would do if she had to give it up. That's why she wouldn't. Not for Jason. Not for anything. Clara flung her bag over her shoulder and walked over to the door. She opened the door and stepped into the reception area of the center. She breathed a sigh of relief when she saw Sandra's empty chair. "Good," she thought. "At least I don't have to worry about telling her where I'm going." Clara rushed over to the door, and without looking behind her she left the center.

....

Thirty minutes later, Clara pulled into the parking lot at Romeo's and parked next to Jason's Acura. She looked up and saw him sitting by the window, looking out for her with a big smile on his face. Clara walked into the restaurant. The hostess escorted her to the table where Jason was sitting. Clara liked this restaurant. Everyone knew them here. All of the waiters and even the manager called them the perfect couple. Clara walked slowly to the table where Jason was waiting for her.

He jumped up as she approached the table. "Hi Clara." He hugged her before she could back away. "I'm happy that you could make it."

"Hi Jason. It's good to see you." Clara realized that she really meant it. She missed Jason, but she had never allowed herself to admit it before. Every time she thought about him, she would have a drink, or pick up a book, or turn on the television.

"You look good, Clara."

"So do you." Boy, did he look good.

"Are you hungry?"

"Yes. I think I'll have a salad and some of your pasta if you don't mind." Clara spoke before she could catch herself. That's what they always had when they came here. She wished she had ordered something else.

"Not at all." Jason's smile was as bright as the morning sun. "I'll order my usual, and you can have some." He waved the waiter over and ordered dinner for the two of them. "Clara, we need to talk. About us."

Clara took a sip of water before she answered him. Where was this heading? She didn't know if she could handle this. She wished she had never come. "I don't know if there is an us to talk about. We've been through some tough times lately, and I don't know if we can go back to the way things were."

"Well, I'm not talking about going back." Jason's expression was serious. "As a matter of fact, I would never go back to the way things were between us. I'm getting older. I'm forty now, and I have no kids."

Clara steadied herself for his next words.

"You know that I want to get married. And have kids. And I know how you feel about marriage, so this is not a proposal."

"So why are you telling me all of this?" Clara didn't understand. If this man knew that she didn't want to get married and he was ready for marriage and children, why was he wasting his time telling her about his dreams?

"Clara, I'm telling you this because I love you. I loved you from the moment we met." Jason started to reach for her hand and then seemed to think better of it. "I thought you were the woman that I would spend the rest of my life with. After you turned down my proposal, I knew that you were really not ready for marriage. Maybe you never will be." He looked into her eyes. "But I am. And I wanted to be sure. If you're not the one, I need to be sure."

Tears filled Clara's eyes as she looked at Jason across the table. She wished that she knew why she couldn't be happy with him. She wanted to marry him, but she was so scared. Then, there was also something else, something that she couldn't quite put her finger on. "Jason, I do love you and I could very easily say that I would marry you, but I know that we would both be miserable if we married each other." Clara looked down at her hands and then back up at Jason again. "Jason, I have too many problems to marry anyone."

"But you could get help."

"I tried that before." Clara laughed through her tears as she wiped them away with her napkin. "I've been to counseling, and my counselor was just as mixed up as I was. She had no clue as to how to help me."

"But Clara, you're a counselor. You're educated about this stuff. Doesn't your knowledge about different issues help you at all?"

"Yes, it does. It helps me to know that I've got problems. It also helps to show me that I can't commit to a lifetime with someone knowing that I have so many hang-ups."

Jason looked confused.

Clara pulled herself together. "Jason, you're a good man, a real man and you need a good woman. You need someone who can love you and appreciate you like you deserve to be loved and appreciated."

She smiled weakly at him. "I'm a little messed up right now, and I need to find help before it's too late."

Jason looked surprised by her confession. Clara had never admitted to Jason before that she needed help. "Look, Clara. There is no other woman out there for me. At least not right now."

"So what are you saying?" Clara wished she had a drink right now. She picked up her glass of water and took a sip.

"What I'm *trying* to say is that I'm not giving up yet. I'm going to wait and see what happens. Don't worry." He spoke before Clara could say anything. "I'm not asking you to take me back and I don't want to move back into the house."

"What do you want then, Jason?"

"That's simple, Clara. I want you to be my wife. If I see that I'm asking for the impossible, then eventually I'll move on."

Move on. Clara didn't like the sound of those words at all.

"In the meantime, just know that I'll be around."

Clara's heart pounded like drums with a jungle beat. She tried to cover her nervousness with a smile. "You'll be around?"

Jason chuckled. Then he looked into her eyes and wrinkled his brow the way he always did when he was serious about something. "Yes, that's what I said. I'll be here when you decide that I'm the man you want to spend the rest of your life with."

Clara shook her head slowly from side to side. Then she stopped and looked right at Jason. "How long Jason?"

He shrugged his shoulders. "I guess only time will tell. Come on. Let's eat this food before it gets cold." He picked his fork up and dug into the dish of pasta that the waiter had just placed in front of him.

Clara watched him for a minute. He was so cute. She loved eating out with him. She smiled as he took her plate and served her some of his pasta. She loved the way he took care of her, always knowing exactly what she wanted. Clara's heart broke all over again as she remembered their fight. She wondered what had happened to the woman that he met the other night. She wanted to ask him about her. But she couldn't. She couldn't bear it if he had been spending time with another woman. She felt like breaking down. Why was her life in such a mess? Clara had to get herself together. She couldn't let him see the pain in her heart. She forced a smile just as he looked up and handed her the plate of pasta.

The Video Store

Hours later, Clara walked into the kitchen of her home and looked around. She grabbed a bottle from the cabinet and sat down at the table with a glass. After pouring a drink and taking a swallow of the amber liquid, she rested her chin on the palms of her hands. Staring straight ahead, she gave a big sigh. She took another swallow and sighed again as big teardrops rolled down her cheeks, hit the table and broke into smaller drops of water. Clara was utterly depressed. What was wrong with her? Why couldn't she just be with Jason and be happy? She thought about the dinner that she'd just had with Jason.

He was so kind and loving. He spent the entire evening looking at her. Every time Clara looked up, he was gazing at her lovingly. At times Jason looked happy to be with her, at times sad, and at other times confused. Clara could see why he was confused. How could any woman in her right mind pass up an opportunity to marry a great guy like Jason? Clara knew women who would jump at the chance to have a man like him. But that was just it. Clara was not like other women, and she was not in her right mind. She had been having problems for a long time. She'd never had a successful relationship. She was afraid to let her guard down. She thought that if she did the guy would realize that he didn't want her after all. She was so afraid of being rejected that she never really let herself love anyone with her whole heart. She kept her fragile little heart locked away inside, not letting any man get close enough to break it.

Time after time, the men in her life would get tired of her coldness and they'd call her names like frigid, ice queen, and cold bitter woman. At this point, Clara always knew what was next. They would leave or she would find a reason to end the relationship. Then she would take comfort in the first bottle of booze that she could get her hands on. Alcohol had become her best friend. When she was alone and drunk, she could just be herself. She would cry her eyes out and drink until she felt better...or passed out. More times than not she just passed out only to wake up next to an empty liquor bottle. Clara knew that she could not go on like this. She had to get some help. She had to find out why she was so afraid to be in a committed relationship.

She had been to counseling before, but her counselor was more messed up than she was. As soon as she found out that Clara was a counselor, she started talking about her own problems. Clara couldn't stop being upset about that one. Here she was paying $80.00 an hour for a counseling session, and the counselor was asking her for advice. The last time Clara was there, she dropped a bill for three hours and one of her business cards on the counselor's desk and walked out. The counselor paid the bill and she was now one of Clara's regular clients.

Clara laughed through the tears that were still falling as she reflected on her attempt to get help. The laughter made her feel better. She got up and grabbed a tissue to wipe her tears. That was enough of that. She wasn't going to sit around crying. She decided to go over to the Video Store and get a movie. It was already after 9:00 but she just couldn't bring herself to go to bed. She got up and headed for the door. A good comedy would help right about now. Before heading out the door, she took another drink and put the bottle back in the cabinet.

....

As Clara pulled into the parking lot of the Video Store, she noticed that there were quite a few cars there. She jumped out of her car and headed inside. As she was rushing into the store, she bumped into a guy who was coming out. "Oops. I'm sorry," she said as she glanced at the man that she had run into.

"Oh, that's okay...Clara?"

"Jeff!"

"Hi Clara. Who would have thought I'd run into you here." Jeff was grinning from ear to ear.

"I know. What a surprise." Clara had not seen Jeff in over two years. She ran her hand over her hair, thinking that she must look a mess. She had not even bothered to check the mirror before she left the house.

"Clara, you look good," the look in Jeff's eyes told Clara that he meant what he said. "But you look a little troubled. Are you okay?"

Clara had always liked this about Jeff. He was always very observant and he seemed to always know when something was on her mind.

"I'm okay. You know how life is sometimes." Clara didn't even try to hide the truth. "I've been having a hard time lately." Her eyes filled with tears and her voice broke. She wiped the tears away and forced herself to smile. "But you look great. How are you?"

Jeff reached out and touched Clara's chin for one moment. "I'm doing really well. I just moved back from Atlanta. You know I started a business down there and it's going really well." He grinned proudly and shoved his hands into his pockets. "I left my partner there to run the shop. And I'll be opening a new office here in New Jersey."

Clara's heart skipped a beat. She couldn't believe that Jeff still had this effect on her. They had broken up when he moved down to Atlanta to start his new business. He had asked Clara to come with him, but she had turned him down.

"Well, it's good to hear that your business is doing well." Clara had always wanted the best for Jeff.

"Oh, and here I was thinking you were going to say that it's good to have me back in town." Jeff half teased her.

Clara giggled like a schoolgirl with a crush. "I see you still have your sense of humor."

"Yeah, you always did laugh at my jokes. That's one of the things I loved about you."

Clara fidgeted under his stare. "Well Jeff, I have to get going. I was just going to stop in and get a movie."

Jeff stepped in front of her to stop her from going. "Listen, I just picked up a great comedy. Why don't we watch it together? I could come to your place or you can stop over to mine. That is, if you're not married or anything?" He glanced at her left hand, smiling when he didn't see a ring.

"No," Clara said. "I'm not married. Far from it." She didn't mean to say that last part.

"Good." Jeff flashed the boyish grin that had once stolen Clara's heart. "Why don't we go ahead and watch this movie together? I've got popcorn." He pulled the popcorn from his bag and waved it in the air.

Clara thought about it. She had really loved Jeff and she still had feelings for him. If they got together to watch a movie, things could get sticky.

"I know what you're thinking," Jeff interrupted her thoughts. "I promise I'll be on my best behavior. Come on, for old time's sake?"

Clara shrugged her shoulders. "Okay. But after the movie is over, that's it. "

Jeff smiled and nodded his head in agreement. "Okay. Your place or mine?"

The Next Day

Clara woke up with a pounding headache. She and Jeff were stretched out on the couch, entangled in each other's arms. She was laying on top of him, with her head on his chest, and his arms were holding her close to him. She was glad she didn't have to go to the Center today. She had scheduled the day off to get her thoughts together. That was before she ran into Jeff. Clara thought back to last night and how natural it had been to curl up in Jeff's arms. They had always been so comfortable with each other.

They came back to Clara's place to watch the movie. Jeff was impressed with the house and complimented her on the way she had decorated. They popped the popcorn and curled up on the couch to watch the movie. The movie was a good one, and Jeff was on his best behavior just as he promised he would be. They sipped wine and ate popcorn. Then they both dozed off.

Clara pulled away from Jeff and looked at the clock. It was already early morning, and she didn't want Jeff to stay any longer. "Jeff," she called as she shook him awake.

Jeff opened his eyes and looked at her. A big grin spread across his face. "I guess we both fell asleep. Why did you wake me?"

The grogginess in his voice was so sexy. Clara watched him as he stretched his arms towards the ceiling.

"This is so comfortable. Come here." He reached out and pulled Clara closer to him. Her heart beat faster as feelings of passion fluttered in her belly.

"Jeff, we shouldn't have spent the night together." Clara pulled away from him and sat up. Just then, she had visions of Jason in the arms of another woman. She wondered if it had been like this for him.

"Why not? It's so good to see you. Nothing has to happen." He reached for her again. "Just let me hold you. Okay?"

Clara's heart did flip-flops in her chest as the fluttering in her belly increased. She thought about how nice it would be to spend more time in Jeff's arms. But she knew that even to innocently continue to cuddle up with him would create problems. "No." She forced herself to stand firm. "Jeff, you have to go. You promised."

Jeff sat up. "Okay Clara Baby."

Clara almost weakened when she heard the nickname that she used to love.

"I'll go. But I'll be back!" He struck his famous body builder pose.

Clara laughed at him. "Jeff, you are so silly."

Jeff bent over to put on his shoes. Standing up he reached out and pulled Clara up from the couch. "I'm glad to see you laugh. I want to see more of that. How about dinner tonight?"

Clara felt the flip-flops in her chest again. "No, I can't. I have plans," she lied.

"Okay, Clara Baby. Look. Here are my numbers." He handed her a card. "Give me a call in a day or so."

"Okay." Clara took the card. "I'll call you."

"Okay, Clara Baby. Have a good day." Jeff leaned in to lightly kiss her lips before he turned and walked out the door.

Clara put her fingers to her lips, still tingling from Jeff's kiss. She couldn't believe it. Jeff Williams was back in town and back in her life. She looked at the card and wondered what she was going to do now.

The Counselor

Later that day, Clara parked her car and looked around before she got out. She wanted to make sure that no one saw her going into the Private Counseling Center. Clara hadn't been to counseling in over a year. She'd thought that by helping other women to solve their problems, she would somehow begin to get better. The only problem was that she didn't seem to be helping anyone. Patricia was still being beat black and blue by her husband and Lauren was still in a relationship with the man that had dumped her three times for other women. Most of her other clients were having a tough time dealing with reality. And her newest client, Jennie was more mixed up than all of them. The women that came to her all had issues that were becoming impossible for Clara to deal with.

Clara walked into the private offices and gave her name to the receptionist. Then she went over and took a seat. She couldn't believe that she was at another counseling center. But she knew that she needed help, and she was willing to give it one more shot.

"Clara Walton." Clara jumped in surprise as she heard her name called. She had expected to wait awhile before she saw someone. She stood up and walked over to the lady who had called her name.

"Hi, I'm Justine Carroll." The woman extended her hand.

"Hi, I'm Clara." Clara felt silly telling this woman her name when she already knew it.

"Welcome to PCC, Clara. Come on in." Justine gestured for Clara to follow her. They walked into a very tranquil area. Clara looked around at the greens and blues that they'd used to decorate the offices. There were paintings of women relaxing under trees, walking in the park, and having tea on the deck. There were also paintings of beautiful landscapes. Clara heard waterfalls and as she looked around, she saw that there was a small waterfall in the center of the inner foyer of the office. She followed Justine into a blue room and sat down on a plush, comfortable sofa. Justine sat down in a chair next to the sofa and crossed her legs. Clara realized that there was no desk in this room. She looked on the wall above the fireplace and noticed a painting of a man dressed like a shepherd. What a beautiful piece of art. There were people crowded all around him and a woman had fallen at his feet, reaching for the hem of his robe. Clara couldn't stop looking at this painting. It was beautifully done in the same vibrant colors that had been used to decorate the counseling center.

"I see you like my painting."

"Yes, it's very nice." Clara was still staring at the painting.

"It's one of my favorites."

Clara just nodded her head.

"What do you think it means?"

"Well, when I first saw it, I thought that maybe it portrayed how women fall at the feet of men their whole lives."

Justine nodded. "Go on."

Clara stared at the painting again. "Then when I looked at his face, I saw that he seemed to be genuinely concerned about the woman at his feet. And I felt a sense of comfort."

Justine smiled. "That's a very good interpretation of the painting, Clara."

"Thanks."

"Okay now. Why don't we talk about you a little bit? What brings you here?"

Clara almost laughed. Justine had to be joking. What brings you here? What would bring anyone to a counseling center? Now she knew how her clients felt when she asked them that question. "Well, I'm kind of mixed up." Clara's eyes darted around the room and then back to look at Justine. She wondered if she could trust her. "I have these issues, and I think I need some help."

"Okay. That's a good start. Why don't you tell me all about it?" Justine shifted her weight and sat back in her chair.

"What?" Clara blinked in confusion. "Don't you have to ask me some questions, to try to get to the main reason for my problem?"

"No, Clara. I'm not going to psychoanalyze you. I want you to tell me about yourself. You can start from when you were a little girl."

Clara felt herself tense up. She didn't know what Justine was trying to do. She didn't want to talk about when she was a little girl. "I don't want to talk about my childhood." She wrung her hands. "My childhood is over. I have adult issues. I need to talk about my life as it is now." Clara didn't know why she was so upset. She felt trapped. She wondered how she could get out of there.

"Okay." Justine's voice was calm. "Tell me about your life as it is now."

Clara stared at Justine. What did she think she was doing? Clara had not expected things to go like this. She had thought that she would be able to control the direction of the session, only revealing what she wanted to. But Justine seemed to have other plans for her. She was trying to make her talk.

"Well," Clara began. "I'm 36 years old and I'm a counselor. I work downtown at the Women's Crisis Center...and I have a lot of clients."

"Unh-huh." Justine calmly nodded her head.

They come in to me with all sorts of problems. Some of them have been coming for months, some a year, but I don't seem to be helping them any."

"Why do you think that is?"

"I don't know. They come in with the problems and they leave with the same problems." Clara thought for a moment. "I think it may have something to do with the fact that I have so many problems of my own. I always feel like a fake, trying to help people when my own life is in such a mess. Whatever it is, I just don't seem to be reaching these women."

"That's good Clara. It's hard to help someone else to walk when you're crippled too."

"Crippled?" Clara had never heard it put that way before.

"Yes crippled. Clara, why are you crippled?"

"What?" Just as Clara had thought, this lady was a little strange.

"Crippled, Clara. That's when something has gone wrong somewhere in your life and that thing keeps you from having a happy life. It normally occurs in childhood and crippled people usually have trouble with relationships."

Of course all of this made sense to Clara. But Clara didn't see how it could help her.

"Clara, the only way that you're going to get better is to face what's making you sick." Justine said looking at her intently.

Clara liked Justine. There was something soothing about her, with her calm manner and gentle voice. Clara wondered if she had any issues of her own. "That's easy for you to say." Clara looked around the room again thinking that she liked this place.

"That's true," Justine interrupted her thoughts. "But only because I know what you're going through. You might not believe it but I used to have many problems of my own." Justine played with the pad in her lap as she told Clara about her past. "I was all messed up. I had issues with my mother, my father, all of my sisters and brothers and any man who ever looked my way."

Clara wondered if she was going to have another episode of reverse counseling.

Justine put the pad on the coffee table and sat forward in her chair. "I refused to face my problems, and they continued to ruin my life. I was drinking, doing drugs, having sex with any man who wanted me, and just running myself into the ground."

Clara had never heard a counselor bare her soul like this before. "So, did you ever face up to your problems?"

"Oh yes. And now I have a peace like none I've ever known."

"What happened?"

"One day I decided that I was sick and tired of my life the way it was. I had been to see counselors and none of them were able to help me."

Clara could identify with that.

"Then one day I met a woman who had so much peace and joy. I asked her what her secret was and she told me. My life hasn't been the same since."

"What was her secret?" Now Clara was sitting on the edge of her seat.

"God." Justine said.

"God?" That was the last thing Clara expected Justine to say.

Justine nodded her head. "She took me to her church. When I walked in the door, I felt a peace like I've never felt before. Because I was reluctant to give up my selfish ways, I visited this church for a few months before I finally joined."

Clara was trying to figure out what Justine was talking about. She knew plenty of people who went to church, and most of them were as crazy as she was. God didn't seem to be helping any of them. In fact, some of them turned to the bottle just like she did to drown their sorrows. Drinking and cursing and everything else. What was this lady talking about?

"I know a lot of people who are religious," Clara said. "Most of them are as sick as I am."

"I can believe that. You see. It's not the religion that makes the difference. It's the relationship with God." She pointed at the painting. "Look at that painting again, Clara. That man represents the Savior. The woman at his feet has had an issue for many years. He is her last hope. She is crawling on the ground because she would be stopped if anyone saw her trying to touch him. He knows that she is there and he cares about her. He cares about her and he cares about her issues. Actually, he's the only one that can help."

Clara looked sideways at the painting, wondering if she had come to the right place.

"I know that you did not come here to talk about God, but you have come to the right place."

Just then Clara thought that Justine must be psychic.

"I realize that you came to talk about your problems and we'll get to that." Justine sat there with her hands clasped. "I just wanted to share with you how God has changed my life, that's all." She leaned back in her chair again. "Now tell me some more about yourself."

Clara opened up then and she and Justine sat and talked for over an hour. When Clara left the Private Counseling Center, she felt better than she had felt in a long time. She was glad that she had found this place. As she drove home, she sang along with the music on the radio, happy to have finally found someone she could talk to about her problems.

Patricia

The next day Patricia came into Clara's office. She had one leg in a cast, which she draped across the couch. She had a black eye and a sling on her right arm. She looked like the cartoon character who always got hit by a falling boulder, trying to catch that bird. This was the worst that Clara had seen her. Her husband had really crossed the line this time. The neighbors called the police this time, and they took Brian away.

Clara tried to make sense of the words that were coming out of Patricia's mouth.

"The...they won't let him out on bail. I have to find a way to get him out."

Clara almost yelled at the woman. Then she remembered that this was a professional relationship.

"Patricia, the man almost killed you this time. Tell me. Why would you want to bail him out?"

"Oh no. He's sorry that he hurt me." Patricia looked as crazy as she sounded. Besides the panicked expression on her face, her hair was all over her head and her eyes were bloodshot. Her face was streaked with tears and her makeup was smeared. "He says that I made him do it when I talked back to him."

"Hello." Clara couldn't hold back any longer. "Patricia, the man is dangerous. Dan...ge...rous. Can't you see? Each time he beats you, it gets worse. Are you going to let him kill you?"

Patricia's eyes welled up with tears. "He's all I have. Clara, he's my whole life."

"I hear what you're saying. But Patricia, have you looked at yourself in the mirror?"

"It's all my fault." Patricia ignored Clara's question and wiped her nose with the back of her hand.

Clara wondered if Patricia was on drugs or something that she couldn't see that Brian was close to killing her.

"If I would have just listened to Brian and not talked back, he wouldn't be sitting up in that stinking jail house."

Clara wished she knew the words to say to reach her client. This girl was playing with fire by staying with Brian. She sat back and stared at Patricia. "Patricia, what is the real reason that you stay with Brian?" Clara could not afford to let Patricia go and bail Brian out. She had to find a way to stop her. "Listen, I know that this is hard for you. But, I need to know about your childhood." Clara took her time. "Patricia, did your father beat your mother?"

Patricia cried harder.

Clara hoped that she would not become hysterical again. Each time they talked about her childhood, Patricia started weeping hysterically.

"Patricia?" Clara had to go on. For Patricia's sake she couldn't quit.

"Yes." Patricia suddenly stopped wailing although the tears were still falling silently down her cheeks. She spoke in a quiet voice. Clara had to strain to hear her. "My father beat my mother. Every time they got drunk, or every time one of us kids acted up, he beat her."

Clara tried not to move too fast. She had never been able to get an answer to this question before. "Okay Patricia. Did your mother ever fight your father back? Did she ever leave him?" Clara leaned on the edge of her seat and waited for an answer.

"No, my mother said that Daddy beat her because she wasn't a good wife." Patricia's voice was clearer now, louder.

Clara shook her head and thought, "What was this? Some kind of generational curse?"

Patricia looked up at her with tears in her eyes. "My mother said that she couldn't leave my father." She was crying openly now. "She said that he beat her because he loved her. She said that all men who love their wives beat them from time to time."

Clara couldn't believe what she was hearing. "Patricia, are your mother and father still together?"

Patricia covered her eyes with her good hand. Through the sobs, her answer was loud and piercing. "No, I don't want to!"

"What, Patricia?" Clara probed further.

"No, I can't!" Patricia's sobs shook her body. "I won't. I can't!"

Clara knew that she should stop here. She was not supposed to push a client over the limit, but she had to go on. There were no limits that she would not cross to save Patricia's life. "Patricia, why aren't your mother and father still together? You said that she would never leave him. You said that she would stay with him forever."

"Noooo."

"What happened, Patricia? Where are your parents?"

"They're dead! They're dead! They're dead!" Patricia yelled at Clara. "My father beat my mother one day...and she threatened to leave him." She moved her hand from her eyes and stared at Clara as though seeing her for the first time.

Clara wondered if she had gone too far. Then Patricia started to speak. Her voice was different. Not like Clara had ever heard it before.

"One day my mother threatened to leave my father and he shot her with his gun...and...then. He shot himself." Patricia sank into the couch. "I was right there. I was so scared. I thought he would kill me too. I wish he had killed me too. It was all my fault."

Clara looked sadly at Patricia. She had no idea that this was what had been haunting her. "Listen, Patricia. None of this is your fault."

"Yes it is. They had been fighting about me. I was seventeen and they had just found out that I was pregnant." She was still crying. "Daddy was getting the belt to beat me and Mommy stopped him." Tears flowed like a waterfall down her face. "Then he started hitting her and that's when she said that she was leaving. Then...he grabbed his gun and shot her." Patricia wailed like a wounded animal. "I killed my parents."

Clara got up and walked over to Patricia. She sat on the edge of the couch and wrapped her arms around her client. "What happened to your baby?"

"My baby's dead. After my parents died, I tried to kill myself. Only it didn't work. But I killed my baby instead. I killed my parents and my baby." Patricia's cries of agony vibrated off the walls of Clara's office. "I deserve to die too." She sobbed so hard they both shook.

Clara didn't say a word. She just rocked Patricia back and forth, back and forth, like she was a baby.

Heart Attack

"Client came in on crutches, with bandages all over and a sling on right arm." Clara dictated into her recorder after Patricia had left. "Beaten by husband who has been..."

"Clara, you have an important call on line one," Sandra interrupted her over the intercom.

Clara wondered who it could be. Sandra knew not to interrupt her when she was recording a client's charts.

"Hello," she barked impatiently into the receiver of the phone.

"Clara..."

Clara sat up straight in the chair at the sound of her sister's voice.

"Clara, you'd better get to Valley Hospital."

"Why, Loretta? What's wrong? Are you okay?" Clara felt sick in the very pit of her stomach.

"No, Clara. It's our mother."

"What's wrong with Momma?" Clara didn't care if she sounded hysterical. "Why is Momma in the hospital?"

Loretta sighed. "Clara, I think you'd better hurry up and get to the hospital." She sounded like she was running out of patience with her sister. "Momma just had some sort of heart attack or something, and she looked pretty bad when they took her out of here."

"Heart attack? Heart attack!" Clara screamed into the phone. "Her heart is fine. She couldn't have had a heart attack!"

"Okay. So I don't know what I'm talking about." Loretta sucked her teeth. "Look. I have to go."

"Wait..."

It was too late. Loretta had already hung up the phone.

Clara dropped the phone and grabbed her keys. She had to get to the hospital before her mother.....No. That was crazy. Her mother wasn't going to die. She probably just had some indigestion or something, or maybe just a small stroke. Loretta must be drunk. Her mother's heart was fine.

"Please God, don't let it be a heart attack," Clara prayed as she headed for the hospital.

Clara ran into the emergency room and stopped at the desk. "I need to see Theresa Walton...she's my mother...I need to see her now..."

The clerk behind the desk held up his hand. "Miss, please slow down."

Clara wanted to scream, "Slow down! My mother just had a heart attack!" She took a deep breath. "Listen, my mother just had a heart attack. Her name is Theresa Walton."

The guy looked down at his pad and gestured towards the emergency ward flaps. "Go right through there. Your mother is in there."

Clara ran towards the gray flaps and rushed through them frantically looking for her mother. A nurse stopped her and asked if she could help. "It's my mother. They say she had a heart attack." As she spoke, Clara could see her mother lying in a bed hooked up to a bunch of machinery. She had a mask over her face that was pumping air into her lungs and a machine that kept making a lot of beeping sounds. She had a tube down her throat and a whole bunch of other tubes all over her body. Clara's legs wobbled beneath her. "Mom." She mouthed the word but nothing came out. "Mom." This time the word was muffled. "Mom!" Clara screamed just before she fainted.

....

Clara woke up to the smell of medicine. She hated that smell, but not as much as she hated hospitals. As she heard the beep beep beep of the machine, she remembered that her mother was here in the hospital because they said she had a heart attack. She opened her eyes and saw her mother still hooked up to all of those machines, with tubes coming all out of her. Her mother looked like she was pretty sick.

"Ms. Walton, I see that you're awake," the nurse said as she approached her. You fainted downstairs in the emergency room. Are you okay?"

Clara reached up to touch her head. She felt like her head was going to burst wide open. "Yeah, is my mother okay?" Clara needed to know that her mother was going to be all right.

"Your mother had a coronary attack. It's pretty bad." The nurse walked over and checked the tape on the monitor. "This is ICU."

"ICU?" Clara thought, the nurse was right. This was pretty bad.

"Your mother is in a coma. She's been this way since she came in."

Clara was glad that she was sitting down. "Will she be okay?" she asked again.

"The doctor will be in shortly to talk to you. Are there any other relatives?"

Clara nodded.

"Then you may want to call them."

Clara nodded again as the nurse left the room. She got up and walked over to the side of the bed and looked down at her mother.

"Mom, what happened?" Clara took her mother's hand, surprised by how lifeless it was, she placed it back on the bed. "Mom, you said that you were going to be okay. You promised." Clara could not hold back the tears that flowed from her eyes.

Her mother just lay there, not even breathing for herself. Clara felt lost. What would she do if her mother died?

"Ms. Walton?"

Clara looked up as she heard her name. The man that headed towards her was handsome. He looked like a doctor from one of those television series. Clara wished that this was a dream. She would give anything to be watching him on TV now.

"My name is Dr. Larson. I'm the attending physician." He reached out his right hand. After Clara shook his hand, he continued. "Ms. Walton, your mother is pretty bad off. Do you know if she had been having problems with her heart?"

Clara shook her head from side to side. "No...not that I know of."

"Well, it looks like her heart was seized by some sort of virus. But it had to be already weak to have been impacted so badly." The doctor's words sounded like they were coming to her through a tunnel. "Your mother is in a coma. Her heart is malfunctioning and we're also concerned about her brain. It's swollen to four times its normal size, and on top of that, she's barely breathing."

Clara tried to figure out in her mind what this meant. It sounded like her mother was dying.

"Technically, your mother is beyond our help. The machines are playing a big part in keeping her alive right now. Do you know how she feels about life support?"

Again Clara shook her head. She had never talked about anything like that with her mother.

"Well, as I said, that is the only thing helping her right now. As the next of kin, you have the right to discontinue it."

Clara couldn't believe what this doctor was saying. Her mother wasn't dead. Her mother was alive. She could see her breathing. She was not going to stop the life support and kill her mother. No matter what the doctor said. The doctor was handing her a form.

"Here is a form that you'll need to fill out. You have to decide what you want to do."

She could tell that he was trying to sound as soothing as possible.

"It's not advisable to leave the life support on for too long. After a few days of being in a coma, a patient begins to deteriorate. After that, even if the patient pulls through, there's a chance he or she could be a vegetable. You have to consider if your mother would want to live like that." He let out a breath as if he was glad that he got that all out.

"Okay." Clara didn't care what the doctor said. She was not going to sign her mother's death sentence. "I'll look at this." She held the form to her chest.

"Okay. If you need me, just have one of the nurses page me." He turned to walk away.

"But, wait..." Clara grabbed at his white jacket. "Can't you help my mother? Can't you wake her up?"

Facing Clara again, the doctor shook his head. "That is going to take a miracle. I'm sorry." He turned from her and rushed out of the room.

A miracle? A miracle? Clara didn't even know exactly what that was. "Oh God, please save my Mother!" she cried out to the heavens. "Please God, don't let my mother die. Not like this, God. Not like this." Clara stood over her mother's bed and held her limp hand. She stood there for what seemed like hours and prayed and prayed and prayed. She didn't know much about praying, but she remembered the picture of the lady in her counselor's office who was crawling to reach the only one who could help her.

She remembered the concerned look on the man's face, and she knew that he cared. She knew that he cared about her and about her mother. So she called out to God and asked him to help her and to help her mother. She even asked him to help her sister and to bring her sister to the hospital. As she was praying, she heard her name. She looked up and almost fainted again when she saw her sister.

"Thank you, God." Clara's whisper was barely heard above the noise of the hospital equipment that was keeping her mother alive. "Hi Loretta." Her voice was louder this time, though strained from crying so much.

"Hi Clara. How is she?" Loretta inched towards the bed as if she was approaching a bed of snakes.

"Loretta, Momma is not doing too good. I've been praying for God to help her."

Loretta's eyes darted from her mother's still form to Clara's face. "Praying?"

Clara reached out her hand to her sister. "Loretta, come over and talk to Momma."

Loretta shook her head. She looked like she would run if Clara took one step in her direction. "I can't, Clara. I've been so horrible to Momma." Tears rolled down her cheeks. "Clara, I wasn't coming here tonight." Just then she swayed from one side to the other. That and the slur in her voice told Clara that she had been drinking. "I went out and tried to drink it all away. I had drink after drink after drink and all I could see was how pale Momma looked when they took her away." Loretta's tears fell like the rain, yet she did not wipe them away. "I thought I hated

"Momma. I thought...I hated her. But I don't. Oh God. Why Momma?"

Clara went over to her sister and put her arms around her. "Loretta, Momma is going to be okay."

Loretta pushed Clara away from her. "No. She's not going to be okay. She's going to die. I spoke to the doctor. He told me. He gave you the papers."

Clara backed up a step and looked at her sister. She couldn't believe that doctor. How could he give up on her mother? She wasn't going to die. She couldn't. "Momma is not going to die." *Die. Die. Die.* The word bounced in Clara's head like a boomerang, cutting her to the core.

"Clara, we have to sign the papers. Momma is going to die, and if she doesn't die, she'll be a vegetable. Momma won't want to live like that."

"No! We're not taking Momma off of life support. I know she'll be fine. She's going to live!" Something stirred deep inside of Clara. She really believed that her mother was going to live. She had prayed and asked God to help her and she knew that he would. "Momma is going to live."

"I only wish that was true." Her sister looked like a scared little girl just then. "I only wish that was true." With those words, Loretta turned and left the room.

A Prayer And A Wish

A few days later, Clara sat and looked around at all of the pretty flowers sent by friends and well-wishers. She gazed across the room at the people surrounding her mother. She wished that this had never happened. Clara wanted her mother to be home, healthy and whole. She sighed as she stood and walked over to the people surrounding her mother. "Doctor, how is she?"

Dr. Larson shifted his attention to her and smiled. "Well, it looks like you got your miracle. Your mother is breathing 85 percent on her own. Her heart is beating again, and she seems to have suffered minimal damage to her brain from being in the coma. The swelling is all gone." He scratched his head. "I've never seen anything like it. The medical board wanted me to bring the students by so that they can see for themselves."

Clara smiled at the doctor. "If this is what a miracle is, then I thank God for it."

"Ms. Walton, are you and your mother religious people?" One of the students piped in.

Clara shook her head. "No, I can't say that we ever gave much thought to religion before. But when the doctor told me that it was going to take a miracle for my mother to live, I began to pray like I have never prayed before. I prayed and I prayed for hours on end. I prayed for my sister to come, and she did. I prayed for God to save my mother from death. I prayed for two days. And on the third day, just when I was about to give up, her fingers moved."

The students were intently listening to Clara's story.

"My sister thought I was crazy, praying to God all of a sudden, but I couldn't stop." Clara cried tears of joy. "Deep down inside of the pit of my belly, I knew that God heard me and I knew that he was going to keep my mother alive."

Dr. Larson shook his head. "Ms. Walton, I have to say that I don't really believe in all of this God stuff. But I believe that your mother experienced a miracle of some kind. Medically she was considered dead." He thought for a minute and asked, "What about your sister? Did she pray too?"

"No." Clara shook her head. "No, but she said that she wished that my prayers would come true and that our mother would live." She stopped and thought for a moment and then continued, "Doctor, all we had was a prayer and a wish. Just a prayer and a wish."

The doctor shook his head again in disbelief. Clara knew that he was confused and she probably should have been too. But all she could think about was how God had saved her mother from the hands of death and for that, she was grateful. "Well, doctor. I'm just glad that my mother got another chance at life." Clara noticed that her mother was awake. "Now, if you'll excuse me, I have to see about her." Clara left the doctor standing there holding his clipboard to his chest. He looked like he was deep in thought, still trying to find some logic to this mystery.

"Momma, I see you're awake. Are you rested?"

"Rested? How long have I been laying up in this hospital bed?" Her voice was still weak.

"Three days, Mom. You were pretty bad off."

Her mother tried to get up but fell back on the pillow in defeat. "Get me out of this bed."

"No. The doctor says you have to rest. You've been through a lot."

"You know I hate hospitals."

Clara took a deep breath. Was her mother crazy? Didn't she know that she could have died? Just then, Clara felt like going home.

"Momma, you'll go home in a day or so. In the meantime, you need to relax."

"Where's your sister. I swear that girl doesn't care anything about me."

"That's not true. She was here when you woke up. Don't you remember?"

"No. I don't. And I don't believe she was here. You're just sticking up for her. She's probably out partying somewhere."

"Look, Momma. Don't go getting yourself all worked up. Loretta went home to change. We've both been with you the whole time. She'll be back."

"I don't know if I want her to." Her mother tried to reach the remote on the table.

Clara picked it up and handed it to her.

One by one, her mother flicked through the channels on the TV. "She's always picking fights with me. You would think she hates me. Probably wishes I had died."

Clara was getting tired of listening to her mother's rambling complaints. "Loretta was very happy to see that you're okay."

"Humph." Her mother frowned and folded her hands across her chest.

Clara had to get out of there. Obviously, her mother was fine. How could she still be complaining about every little thing? Why wasn't she grateful to be alive? "Momma, I think I'll run home for a few minutes." Clara pulled at her clothes. "I've had on the same clothes for three days. I need to go home and take a shower and check on the house."

For a moment, her mother's eyes sparkled with fear. "So, you're going to leave me too. What if I have a relapse? No one will be here."

"The doctor said you'll be fine." Clara put her hand to her own chest and took a deep breath. She had never been claustrophobic before. All of a sudden, she felt that the walls and the windows, along with all of the furniture in the room, were closing in on her. There was a constant beeping and whirring in her head from the machines. Her mother's body, the bed, even the windows, attacked her from all angles. She felt herself slipping. She walked over to her mother and kissed her on the cheek. "I'll be back, Mom. You'll never miss me."

Her mother's hand moved as if to grab Clara's hand. Then she let it drop back on the bed. "Okay." Her voice was barely above a whisper now.

Clara headed for the door before she could change her mind. "I'll be back as soon as I can." She kept moving out the door and into the hallway. She ran down the corridor to the elevator. Once there, she pounded the button until the elevator stopped on her floor. When the doors opened, the elevator was full. Clara squeezed into the elevator, ignoring the dirty looks from the people already there. They didn't understand. She couldn't bear to be in that place one more moment. Standing in the crowded elevator, she breathed deeply. In and out. In and out. Until the elevator finally reached the lobby. She bolted out of the elevator, leaving curiosity and speculation in her wake.

Who's That Lady?

A minute later, Clara stood outside and breathed in deeply of the fresh air. She hadn't seen the sunlight for three days. She needed a shower and some fresh clothes. As she stood there in the hospital parking lot, her stomach growled. Clara realized that she was starving. She had not eaten much in the past few days. She needed to get something to eat, but she didn't dare go anywhere looking like this. She was a mess. Clara drove home and jumped into the shower. After pulling on a pair of jeans and a sweatshirt, she went into the kitchen to see what she had to eat. "Empty," she thought as she stood looking into the refrigerator. Feeling like she would die if she didn't eat soon, Clara got into her car and drove for a little while. She pulled over into the parking lot of Applebee's. As she parked the car, she thought of Jason. This had been one of their favorite places. Before she could change her mind, she got out of the car and entered the restaurant.

While waiting to be seated, she looked around at the couples that were also waiting. They all seemed so happy and so in love as they laughed and talked and shared tender touches. She and Jason used to be like that. She had always loved coming here to eat with him. They would sit and laugh and talk for hours. She had always felt special when they were together. She wondered how Jason was. She had not spoken to him during this whole ordeal. She made up her mind to call him today when she got a chance.

As the hostess was taking her to her table, she heard a familiar laugh. She stopped in her tracks and looked down at Jason and a very pretty woman sitting at the table that she was passing.

"Clara." Jason sounded surprised as he looked up at her.

"Hi Jason." Clara's heart was beating too fast.

"Clara, what are you doing here? I mean. I've been trying to reach you. Where have you been?"

Clara forced back an angry response. She didn't want him to see how hurt she was. "Jason, I have to go." She turned and headed for the door. Then she stopped and turned to face them again. "Jason, who is that woman?"

"Uhh. Oh. Clara, this is Monica." Jason looked really uncomfortable. "She's a friend of mine."

"Oh. Okay. I have to go now, Jason. Nice meeting you, Monica." She turned and ran out of the restaurant before Jason could stop her. She got in her car and started the engine. As she drove away, she could see Jason in her rearview mirror. He had come out after her. He had a lot of nerve. While her mother was in the hospital nearly dying, he was out having fun with some woman.

Clara realized that she was crying. She wondered who the woman was. She wondered if this was the same lady that Jason had met the night of their fight. The two of them had been having such a good time Clara realized that she really missed those times of laughter and conversation with Jason. She felt sick. She had really messed things up now. Now Jason had another woman in his life. Who was she? Monica. Even her name was pretty.

Clara drove and drove. She didn't know where she was going. She really had no place to go. She had lost the only man who ever really loved her. The one man that she had been able to be herself around, except for the drinking. Jason thought that she had an occasional drink, but Clara had been careful to hide the fact that she had been drinking every day. At that moment, she vowed that she wouldn't interfere with Jason's happiness. She had blown her chance to be with him. He deserved to be happy and she would not go crying for him to come back to her.

Clara cried and cried and cried. Her heart was broken into little tiny pieces. Jason had another woman. But he had said that she was just a friend. Clara's sense of reasoning tried to push its way through. No, that is what all men say when they have been caught in the act.

"Who's that woman?"

"Oh she's just a friend."

Clara was crying so hard she had to pull over to get herself together. She opened the glove compartment and reached for a tissue to dry her eyes. As she started to close the door, she spotted the bottle of booze that she had stashed in there. She knew that she shouldn't drink on an empty stomach, but she needed something to ease the pain. "I'll just have a little bit," she told herself as she opened the bottle and took a long swallow. She leaned her head back against the headrest and took another swallow, enjoying the sensation of the liquor burning in her chest and flowing into her stomach. After a few more swallows of the warm, soothing, liquid, Clara felt warm all over. She embraced the bottle like she would an old friend. Holding the bottle in her lap, Clara started the car and headed home.

It's Not What You Think

Clara put the key in the lock and dropped her stuff on the kitchen table. Still holding her bottle of booze from the car, she got a glass from the cabinet and headed for the living room. "It's just you, me and the TV," she said to the bottle in her hand as she picked up the remote control and turned the television to her favorite station. Flopping down on the couch she poured herself a drink.

Clara sat in front of the television drinking and watching a rerun on television. She had seen this one before. It was about the woman who lived with her crazy mother. The mother was very controlling and wouldn't let the daughter have any kind of personal life. So she snuck out once a week to go to this bar to meet her lover. On the way to the bar, she stopped at a service station and changed from a mousy, homely girl into a sexy seductress. She also used another name at this bar. She and her lover would have drinks and then go to a hotel room to make love. One night her lover wanted to know who she really was, so he looked into her wallet while she was in the shower. The next day, he showed up at her doorstep. There she stood, no sexy dress, no makeup and scared to death that her mother would find out about her lover and that her lover would find out about her crazy mother. The thing that she fears the most happens when her mother comes out and invites the man in for dinner. Before the meal is over, her lover knows all about her double life. He calls her nuts and leaves, never to be seen again. The woman spends the rest of her life taking care of her mother, never finding real love.

That was the story of Clara's life, except for the part about the crazy mother. Her family was dysfunctional enough though. That's why she couldn't let her guard down. Any man that knew about her secrets would be sure to leave her and never come back. So she never let anyone know. She just lived with this thing year after year, all the time pretending to have it all together. In public, she was a cool, confident woman. But behind the veil, she was scared, sad and suffering. She was getting tired of her life being a television movie. She wondered where the writers got their material. Then she remembered that these were real life women with real life issues.

Clara sat on the couch and watched movie after movie about women whose lives had gone wrong. She would doze off while watching one movie and wake up to another and another. Each story seemed to be sadder than the last.

Why did so many women have to suffer so much? And most of them at the hands of men? That was

Clara's problem now. She had never believed in men. Not since her father had let her down. Sometimes she felt like she hated men. She just wanted to hurt them like she had been hurt. She knew that she would never marry and she definitely would never have children. Yet deep down in her soul, she wished that her life was different. Clara got up from the couch and turned off the television.

"Okay girl, enough of that," she told herself as she headed for the stairs. "You don't have time to sit around and dwell on that mess." She looked at the clock. It was 6:30 in the morning. She had been up all night watching TV. During the night, she had dozed off a couple of times and she hoped that those naps would help her to make it through the day at work today. It was a good thing that she didn't have to go in until ten. Maybe she could sleep for another couple of hours. She got undressed and pulled a nightgown on over her head. Then she curled up under the covers. Just as she was dozing off, the doorbell rang.

At first, Clara thought that she was dreaming. After all, who would be ringing her bell at this time of the morning? "Momma," she thought as she jumped up and ran downstairs to answer the door. Praying that it wasn't someone bringing her more bad news about her mother, she flung open the door and was relieved, surprised, and angry to see Jeff standing there holding an overnight bag with a stupid grin on his face.

"Clara, I'm sorry I woke you up." He moved closer to her. "I need to use your shower. The pipes burst at my place, and I have a very important meeting this morning at 8:00."

Clara looked at him like he was crazy. What kind of trick was he trying to pull with that old line?

"I know this sounds like an excuse for me to come over here and take my clothes off." Jeff knew her like a book. "But I promise you, I'm telling the truth. You can even call my landlady. She lives on the first floor."

"Okay, come on in." Clara stood back to let him walk by.

"Thanks, Clara Baby." Jeff's eyes drank in the sight before him.

Clara realized that she was standing there in her nightgown. She had not even stopped to grab a robe before running down to open the door. "Stop that," she scolded him. "I'll be back. I have to get a robe."

"No, don't." He reached out to stop her. "I like you just the way you are," he said sexily as he leaned down to kiss her lips.

For a moment, Clara lost herself in his kiss. She had always loved the way he kissed her. He was always so gentle with her, always so loving. Except for the times when they had fought. Clara pulled away from Jeff as she remembered his mean streak. That is why she had not gone to Atlanta with him. She had loved him with all she had to give, but he was really mean to her when she didn't do what he wanted her to do. She remembered how he had cursed her out on the day he left for Atlanta.

On the way to the airport Jeff told her that he had a ticket for her. She could come with him and they would send for her things. Clara told him that she couldn't just leave. She said that she would think about it, but that she doubted that she could leave everything behind. He became really angry with her and said some really nasty things to her as she stood there and cried. Then he turned and walked towards his gate without even a backwards glance. Clara had not heard a word from him until she bumped into him at the Video Store that night.

"Hey. Clara Baby. What's the matter?"

The sound of Jeff 's voice brought her back to the present.

"Oh...I was just thinking about something." Clara moved further away from him. "Listen, you'd better get going. You can use the shower upstairs. There are clean towels in the linen closet right outside the bathroom."

Jeff stared at her. "You look strange. Are you sure you're okay?"

Clara nodded her head. "Yes, I think I'm going to be okay. As a matter of fact I'm going to be fine." She got that funny feeling in the pit of her stomach again. She didn't know why, but she was beginning to feel different all of a sudden. What the heck was going on with her lately anyway?

"Okay," Jeff said. "I'm going up to take that shower." He winked at her. "Are you sure you don't want to join me?"

A surge of anger shot through Clara as she shook her head and Jeff turned and went up the stairs. She couldn't believe it. Jeff had done it again. She cringed as she heard him turn on the shower. He thought that he could just come in here before daylight and get into her panties. She didn't believe that he had played her so cheaply. What is the problem with these men? Why do they think that they can treat a woman any kind of way and get away with it? The answer came booming through her mind loud and clear. "Because we let them. That's why they do it. Because we let them."

Clara reached for a kitchen chair and sat down. Wow. That's some revelation. Men treat women badly simply because we let them. Clara knew this. Only this time it hit her like a ton of bricks. She had been a victim all of these years because she had allowed herself to be one. She could use some aspirin and a cup of coffee. Clara got up and put the coffeemaker on. Then she opened the pantry and took out some aspirin. She was on her way to get some water when the doorbell rang. Clara stopped in her tracks and pinched herself to make sure she was not dreaming. She wondered who that could be. She walked over and peeked out to see who it was. She almost fainted when she saw Jason standing there.

"Clara, please open the door. I need to talk to you."

Clara opened the door and stood in the doorway blocking his entrance. "Jason, what are you doing here? It's not even 7:00 in the morning."

"Clara, I've been crazy since I saw you yesterday. I took Monica home and spent the whole night trying not to call your number."

Monica. Clara thought. How could she forget pretty little Monica? "So, what are you doing here?" she asked again.

"Clara, I've been up all night thinking about you. Thinking about us," Jason said as he gently moved her to the side and walked into the kitchen.

"Jason, this is not a good time. I have to get ready for work."

"Clara, you don't understand..." Jason stopped. He looked like he had just seen a ghost. Who are you?" he asked angrily.

Clara turned around and saw Jeff standing there, water glistening off of his hairy chest, with a towel wrapped around his waist. She felt like dying.

"Jason," she said as he moved past her towards the door. "Wait! Jason, wait!" she yelled after him as he opened the door to his car. "Wait, Jason. It's not what you think." She ran barefoot towards his car. "It's not what you think." She stood watching him as he drove away. "It's not what you think," she cried as she sank to the ground in the driveway. "Jason. Stop. It's not what you think. It's not what you think."

Lauren And Tony

Later that day, Clara sat across from Lauren and tried to concentrate on what she was saying. Lauren looked bad. She looked worse than Clara felt if that was possible. Clara had dragged herself in to work after that embarrassing scene this morning. She couldn't believe that she had been sitting in the middle of the driveway in her nightgown. Some of the neighbors had come out of their houses to see what was going on. To top it all off, Jeff had come out in his towel to help her back into the house. Clara chuckled to herself as she thought about what had happened next.

As he was helping her to get up, the towel dropped from around his waist. When they stood upright, there he was in all of his glory, mooning some of the neighbors and saluting others. Clara started laughing uncontrollably when she saw him standing there naked. Jeff grabbed the towel and wrapped it back around his waist, but not before everyone in the neighborhood saw what he had to offer. She laughed as he took her into the house. Then she cried when she realized that she had probably lost Jason forever. Jason thought that she and Jeff were.....oh, it was too horrible to think about. Her laughter turned into a calm anger as she told Jeff to get out and to make sure that he never came back. He went upstairs to get his things. Then he came down and left without a word.

Clara figured that from past experience, he knew that she was serious. She could still remember the puppy dog look on his face when he walked out of her house. Clothes were sticking out of his bag as though he had stuffed them in as fast as he could. Clara chuckled again.

"Clara, why are you laughing?" Lauren asked her. "Are you even listening to me?" Lauren seemed annoyed. "Or do you want me to come back some other time?"

"No." Clara didn't realize that she had laughed out loud. "I'm sorry. I'm totally distracted. I had a rough morning, but everything is going to be okay."

"You won't believe what's going on." Lauren started again. "Tony and I were doing really well. We were finally going to get married."

"Married?" This bit of news immediately won Clara's attention. "The last time you were here, you said that you were just friends."

"I know. I know," Lauren said. "But after I last saw you, Tony convinced me that we should go ahead and get married."

Clara forced herself not to shake her head. She needed to let Lauren talk. "What about your daughter? Was she okay with this whole thing?"

"That's just it," Lauren said. "Tony convinced me not to tell her. He said that it would be better if we just went to the Justice of the Peace and tied the knot and then we could tell her later."

"Oh," Clara said. "And you went along with that?"

"You don't understand. I love Tony so much, and I would do just about anything to keep him."

Clara thought that this woman really had it bad. She was willing to risk her relationship with her little girl over some man.

"Well, we were going to go downtown and get married, but we had to have two witnesses."

"Go on," Clara told her.

"So I asked my sister and Tony asked his best friend. Then I had to have a new dress, and I wanted it to be white."

Clara nodded for Lauren to go on.

"Then on Friday, my sister called me and my daughter answered the phone."

Clara picked up her pencil and twirled it between her fingers.

"My sister didn't know that my daughter didn't know that I was getting married," Lauren said as tears filled her eyes. "So she told her to tell me that she wouldn't be able to come and be a witness for me and Tony to get married."

Clara continued to play with the pencil.

"After that, my little girl hung up the phone and came into the room where I was putting on my new white dress." Lauren wiped at the tears on her face. "She came over to me and started to yell at me."

"What did she say?"

"She said that she hated me." Lauren was sobbing now. "She said that I was a rotten, dirty, liar and that she hated me."

"What happened next?"

"Well, I reached over and tried to calm her down and the doorbell rang and it was Tony."

Clara felt like she was watching television again.

"Tony came in and saw the scene that she was making and he yelled at her to shut up."

"Shut up? Is that what he said to her?" Clara put the pencil down.

"Yes," Lauren sobbed. "But she wouldn't stop yelling at me. She just kept yelling dirty, stinking, liar, dirty, stinking, liar, dirty, stinking, liar until I thought I couldn't take it anymore."

"What finally happened? Were you able to make her stop?"

"Before I could try to stop her, Tony grabbed her and began to shake her, hard."

Clara tried to remain calm as she listened to Lauren tell about what had happened.

"She started yelling at him to let her go, and then." Lauren stopped.

"And then what?"

"He hit my baby. He slapped her so hard that he left his handprint on her face." Lauren's pretty face was twisted with anger. "That bastard hit my baby."

Clara had heard enough. She wanted to tell Lauren that she should have seen it coming, but that wasn't what she was here for. This woman had made a mistake. She had thought that this man was some knight in shining armor when he was nothing but a punk pig. "Lauren, what happened after that?"

"I ran over and began to beat him with my fists screaming at him to let my baby go," Lauren cried. "And then he turned around and started coming towards me with both of his hands balled up into fists. I thought he was going to kill me or hurt me really bad."

Clara just sat there, waiting for Lauren to finish.

"Before he could get to me, I ran into the kitchen and grabbed the biggest knife I could get my hands on. Then I went after him. I really wanted to kill him at that moment." Lauren clenched both fists and thumped them on the Clara's desk. "I wanted to kill the bastard."

"Did you cut him?" Clara asked, hoping that she had.

Lauren shook her head. Her eyes were red from crying and she slumped in her chair. "No. My next door neighbor started banging on the door, asking if we were okay. She wanted to know if she should call the cops. We all just stood there looking at each other. Finally, the bastard opened the door and ran away." Lauren let out a deep breath. "My little girl was just standing there. She looked like she was in shock. I took her to the hospital and they started an investigation to see if I've been abusing her." Lauren started sobbing again. "I told them what happened, and they went to question Tony. I don't know if they locked him up or anything, but they think that I may have somehow been involved in beating my daughter."

Clara was really sorry to hear this. She knew that Lauren would never beat her daughter. But she had gotten involved with the wrong man, and now she was going to have to suffer a little as a result of it.

"Listen, Lauren you're a good mother," she told her client. "You really only wanted the best for yourself and your daughter." She reached over across the desk and handed Lauren another tissue. "We all make mistakes in love. Now you have to move on. If you do what's right for both you and your daughter, this whole thing will pass. You'll get through it and so will your little girl."

Lauren blew her nose and wiped the tears from her eyes. She was looking down at her lap and seemed to be deep in thought about something.

Clara wondered if she had heard her.

"Yeah, I made some mistakes with Tony. I loved him too much. I even loved that bastard more than my daughter, or myself."

Clara sensed a breakthrough. Oh, but what a shame that Lauren's little girl had to be hurt in the process.

"I swear. That's the end of me and Tony." Lauren held up her head and looked right into Clara's eyes. "I will never put some man's needs above the needs of my little girl again. Never."

Clara felt that she meant it. "Where is your daughter?"

"They have her in a foster home. I have to take parenting classes before they'll let her come home.

They have pretty much cleared me of abusing her. After they talked to her, they realized how close we are." Lauren started crying again. "I still have to take those classes, though. And they say they'll let my baby come home after I'm done."

"Lauren, don't worry. Just do what you have to do. Your daughter will be home soon."

Lauren nodded her head. "I don't know how I let this happen. I love that girl more than my own life. I've been so stupid."

Clara nodded. "The good thing is that we can learn from our experiences. You can't be a hostage to your past. You have to move beyond what has happened and try to repair your relationship with your daughter. It's going to be a while before she can trust you again. But kids are pretty forgiving. You have to really show her how much you love her and be the very best mother that you can right now."

Lauren was just sitting there, nodding her head up and down. "I will."

"I know that you will. I really believe that you will."

Private Counseling Center

Clara left her office at lunchtime and headed for the Private Counseling Center. She had called to see if Justine could see her today and was happy when the secretary told her to come on in.

She had been sitting in the waiting room for about ten minutes and was just thinking of leaving and coming back some other time when Justine came out and called her name.

"Hi Clara. It's good to see you." Justine smiled as she reached out to shake Clara's hand. "Come on in."

Clara walked back into the peaceful offices and immediately felt better. There was something about this place that was so peaceful and calming.

"Have a seat." Justine waved towards the seating area.

Clara sat down on the couch and crossed her legs. Justine chose the armchair across from the couch.

"Clara, I haven't heard from you since you were here the last time. Is everything okay?"

Clara liked the way Justine talked to her. It was like she was an old friend, although Clara wouldn't know about old friends. She didn't have any. She could never trust women enough to consider them to be friends. The women that she knew were always making eyes at her man, or gossiping about her or trying to stab her in the back. She remembered how her own cousin had slept with her boyfriend when she was eighteen. Since then, she had decided that she didn't need friends like that, though sometimes she wished that she had a girlfriend that she could hang out with and confide in.

"Clara is everything okay?" Justine repeated her question.

"No. My life is falling apart."

"What happened Clara?"

"Everything. You know that Jason and I broke up. Then Momma had a heart attack, and they thought that she was going to die. Then Patricia comes into my office all beat up and Lauren's boyfriend slapped her little girl." Clara's tears were flowing like a river. "Then I ran into Jeff at the Video Store and we watched a movie together. Jason was having lunch and laughing and having a good time with Monica, and then he came over to my house and Jeff was in the shower." Clara stopped.

Justine got up and picked up a box of tissue. She handed the box to Clara and sat next to her on the couch. "Clara, wow. You have a lot going on. Is your mother okay?"

"Yeah," Clara nodded her head as she looked up at the painting. "Momma is fine. She was in a coma, and they said she was going to die. She couldn't breathe and her heart was all messed up. The doctor wanted me to sign the papers to stop the life support."

Justine's eyes filled with concern as she looked at Clara. "Did you sign the papers?"

"No." Clara shook her head as she looked up at the painting of the man with the woman at his feet. "No. I remembered what we had talked about, and that you said that God was the only one who could save us, and I prayed."

Justine smiled and nodded for Clara to go on.

"I prayed for hours and hours, asking God to save Momma. I didn't care about anything else. I just wanted my mother to live."

"Yes, I can understand that."

Clara wiped her tears with the tissue. "The funny thing is, I think God heard my prayers and answered them. Justine, the doctor said that my mother needed a miracle. I asked God for a miracle, and for some reason he gave it to me. My mother is alive, Justine, my mother is alive."

"Praise God. I am so happy to hear that. Did she go home from the hospital yet?"

"No, they wanted to keep her for observation. I'm taking her home in the morning."

"Clara, that's great, and God answered your prayers because He cares about you. Now tell me about some of these other problems." Justine kicked off her shoes and curled her feet underneath her.

Clara liked her style. She really felt comfortable here. "Well, you know that I kicked Jason out."

Justine nodded.

"Then I saw him in the restaurant with this very pretty lady named Monica." Clara felt better just talking about all of this. "After that Jeff came over to my house to take a shower because he said that his pipes burst and Jason came over and saw him in a towel and thought that we had spent the night together." Clara put her hands in front of her eyes. "It was horrible."

"Clara, do you love Jason?"

"Yes. I love Jason more than I've been able to love any man."

"Clara, what about you?"

"What?"

"Well, what about you, Clara? Do you love your self?"

Clara thought about the question. No one had ever asked her that before. Of course she loved herself. She had to love herself. Didn't she?

"Clara, I'm waiting for your answer. I know that you once loved Jeff and that you love Jason. I know that you love your mother and your sister. You even love your clients. But do you love you. Do you love Clara?"

Clara shook her head. "I don't know. I think I love myself. Yet, I really don't know. It seems that I've never really thought about it."

"Well, you need to think about it because we need to find out why you think you are so unlovable." Justine fixed her eyes on Clara's face. "Could it be that you've never really learned to love yourself unconditionally?"

Clara thought about that for a moment. She thought about the drinking and the men who just seemed to come in and then go out of her life. She thought about her insecurities and how she never really felt worthy of being loved by anyone. She thought about how she hated the way her life had turned out. As she thought about it, she realized that she really didn't think much of herself after all.

"You know, Justine. I don't think that I know how to love myself."

Justine jumped in with the next question. "Clara, at what point did you stop loving yourself? Did something happen?"

Clara saw where this was heading. She didn't want to go there. She fidgeted in her seat. She wanted to get up and run out of Justine's office.

"Calm down, Clara. We're not going to talk about anything that you don't want to talk about," Justine reassured her. "I just want to help you to get better."

Clara nodded her head. "Justine, I have a lot of problems."

Justine just sat there, prompting Clara to go on with her silence.

"I came here because I'm tired of carrying these problems around. I need some help to sort out what's going on with me."

"I'm here for you, Clara." Justine's voice was soothing. "Listen, would you like something to drink? A coke or something?"

"Yes. Diet coke if you have it."

"Okay. I'll be right back." Justine jumped up off the couch and headed out the door without her shoes. Clara sat back on the couch and looked at the painting. She liked this place. She knew that this was the right place for her to get the help she needed. She closed her eyes and tried to think of why she was so messed up.

She thought about her life over the past ten years and realized that it had started even before then, way before then. She thought about her family and started to feel sad. She thought about her sister who was more messed up than she was. She thought about her mother who had been an alcoholic since she could remember. She thought about her father, who had left when she was ten. No, he had not left. Her mother had kicked him out. She tried to remember why her mother had kicked him out. She thought about all of the years of her sister telling her that her father had messed the whole family up and she couldn't figure out why Loretta kept saying this. What was she missing? She tried to remember when her father lived in the house, but she couldn't remember much, only the drinking, and the fighting and the...

"Sorry it took me so long," Justine said as she came back into the room. "Clara, what's wrong?"

Clara realized that she was crying again. "I don't know." She reached for a tissue. "I was thinking about my family, and I guess I just started crying."

Justine was looking closely at Clara. "Clara, do you want to talk about it?"

"No." Clara shook her head as she reached for the diet coke. "I'd rather not." She took a sip of the soda and then put it on the table next to the couch.

"That's okay. Sometimes we work things out with others, and sometimes they're worked out when we're all alone. I sense that your coming here is helping you to take a look at some things that you may have buried." Justine sat down next to Clara. "Listen Clara, there are some dead areas in your life that you may not want to face. These things are preventing you from having the life that you're supposed to have. Until you face them, you will never be able to be totally happy in your life. Hopefully, you can find help like I did and begin to really live."

Clara nodded as she looked at her counselor. "I would like that. I would really like that."

"Don't worry then. If you have a desire to be healed, you will be." Justine put her glass down. "Now Clara, do you mind if we pray?"

"Pray?"

"Yes." Justine nodded her head. "Prayer is part of our therapy here. Didn't you read the brochure?"

Clara shook her head. "No, as a matter of fact, I didn't have a chance to read it."

"Oh. I'm sorry."

"No, don't be." Clara put down her glass. "I would like to pray."

Justine took her hands and they bowed their heads as Justine began to pray. After they finished praying, Clara left. She felt better than she had in a long time. For the first time in a very long time, she felt like her life was worth living.

Momma's Homecoming

The next morning, Clara rolled over and turned off the alarm. She sat on the edge of the bed and stretched her arms towards the ceiling. She got up and headed to the bathroom. After she showered, she put on a pair of slacks and a nice blouse. She wanted to look nice. Momma was going home from the hospital today, and Clara was so happy she felt like singing.

Her mother was almost one hundred percent better. The doctors had kept her an extra day to run additional tests to see if they had missed anything. They were trying to say that they had misdiagnosed her in the first place. The doctors were saying that Momma had not been in critical condition after all and that she had probably only been in shock. Only Clara and Dr. Larson had been able to stand and say that Momma had definitely been near death, and that it had truly been a miracle that brought her out of the woods.

In spite of what Clara and Dr. Larson said, the other doctors didn't want to believe that Momma had been in any real trouble. Clara didn't care what they believed. She knew that her mother had been close to death and that she had been given another chance. She just wanted to take her mother home and let Dr. Larson deal with the other doctors in the hospital.

Before leaving her house, she looked around to see if she was forgetting anything. When she was sure she had everything, she headed for the hospital.

....

A few hours later, as Clara pulled into her mother's driveway, she could see her sister's car and another car that she did not recognize. She wondered who else would be there before her mother even had a chance to get settled. Clara got out and went around to the other side of the car to help her mother. As she and her mother walked towards the house, Loretta flung the door open and came out.

"Welcome home, Momma," she slurred as she stood back to let them in. "It looks like you have a little welcome home present here."

Clara and her mother walked past Loretta into the house. They both stopped in their tracks when they saw who was standing in the room. Clara wanted to run and hide. She couldn't believe that the man who had hurt her so badly when he abandoned her as a child was standing in her mother's living room. "What was he doing here?" Clara thought as she realized she was scared.

"Hi, Theresa." Her father smiled at her mother. "I'm glad to see that you're okay."

Her mother blushed and giggled. "Oh no you're not. It seems like you're trying to give me another heart attack. Surprising me like that."

Clara was screaming, but no sound was coming out. She looked at her sister and saw that she was drunk.

Loretta walked over to the bar and poured another drink.

Clara just stood there staring at her father. She had not seen him since she was ten. What was he doing here? She looked around as if to find a way to escape.

"Hello Clara." Her father reached his arms out to her. "Aren't you even going to give your old man a hug?"

Clara felt like throwing up. It was only now that she realized the intensity with which she hated him. She didn't want to hug him, she wanted to spit in his face and ask him why he had rejected her when she was a child.

"Hi," she said coldly, never leaving her mother's side. "Momma, come over to the couch. You need to lay down."

"Clara, they've had me laying up in that hospital for days. The last thing I want to do is lay down."

Her mother was stubborn. She was usually as tough as nails, but Clara watched with surprise as she blushed like a teenager while she flirted with her father.

"Man, you look like you need a meal. Do you want me to cook you something to eat?"

Loretta looked like she wanted to gag. "Oh, no. I know that I have to get out of here now," she slurred drunkenly. She spun around and faced her mother. "You just got out of the hospital, and you want to go in the kitchen and cook for that man." She pointed at their father.

"Loretta, you're drunk," her mother accused.

"Okay. So do you want to tell me something that I don't know?" Loretta took one step towards their father. "You can start with telling me why he's here." She said pointing both fingers at him. As she backed away from him, she stumbled. She steadied herself and leaned against the couch, never taking her eyes off of their father, who was standing there with a stupid look on his face. Then she stood up again and walked over to her mother. "I come over here to welcome you home, and guess who's coming to dinner comes ringing the bell. And then he comes in here like he was just here yesterday and like he's never done anything to mess up my childhood and to mess up my family." She spun drunkenly around and pointed at their father again. "This man messed up my whole life." She was almost screaming as she finished.

"Loretta, let's go into the kitchen and fix Momma something to eat." Clara tried to calm her sister down.

"No!" Loretta was screaming now as she pushed Clara away from her. "I'm getting out of here. I can't stand to be in the same house with that man. I hate him." She glared at their father. "Did you hear me?"

She yelled at him. "I...hate...you!" She turned and ran from the house.

Clara ran after her. Loretta was in no shape to go anywhere. Clara found her sitting on the porch where she had fallen. "Loretta, are you okay?" Clara kneeled down next to her.

Loretta lifted her head to look at her sister. "Okay?" she growled like an angry bear. "You're asking me if I'm okay?"

"Listen Loretta. Let me help you up. Were you going somewhere?" Clara tried to help Loretta up, but Loretta pulled away from her. Clara sat down on the porch with her legs under her.

"Yeah," Loretta said. "I'm going anywhere that he won't be. How dare he come here? Where did he come from, Clara?" Loretta was crying. "Why is he here? Please tell me he's not going to stay." She begged. "Hey, you can go in there and tell him to leave. They'll listen to you."

Clara shook her head. "Listen Loretta, I know that you can't stand Daddy, but Momma is happy that he's here. Can't you just let him stay for a little while?"

"Are you crazy? Clara, don't you remember what he did to me?"

Clara shook her head. "What are you talking about?"

"Don't you remember what he did?" Loretta asked. "Don't you remember what your father did to me?"

Clara could hear the screams in her head again as she shook her head. "No, I don't know what you're talking about." She felt like throwing up.

"Yes you do, Clara. You have to remember."

Clara was still shaking her head. She didn't want to remember. She didn't want to know. Why was this happening to her? She scrambled to her feet. She had to leave. Now.

"Clara, where are you going?"

"I just remembered. I have to go." She started towards the house. She would just go in and tell her mother that she would come back later.

"No, you can't leave me." Loretta got up and ran over to her. "Clara, don't leave me here with them. Momma hates me and that man...."

Clara let go of the doorknob and turned to go the other way. She felt like she was going in a circle. Tears streamed down her face. What was going on? "Oh God, help me," she prayed silently.

"Clara, stop...just stop!" her sister yelled at her.

Clara stopped and looked at her sister who was holding her to stop her from walking away.

"Clara, that man in there raped me. I was thirteen years old and he had sex with me...Clara." Loretta burst into tears and sank to the ground crying like a baby.

Clara stood staring at her sister for a moment. Suddenly, it all came crashing back to her memory. She sank down on her knees and wrapped her arms around her sister as she remembered the day that her father had left. She remembered it like it was yesterday. Her mother and father had a big fight that day. Clara closed her eyes and then opened them to stop the pictures from flashing through her mind, but the memories kept flashing in front of her eyes.

She saw her mother throw the lamp at her father. Then she threw a chair, and the coffee table. She picked up centerpieces and even threw the dishes from her china cabinet as he ducked each thrown item.

"Get out, you bastard," her mother yelled at him. "You sick bastard! How dare you put your hands on my little girl?"

"No," her father said. "She's lying. I never touched her. You have to believe me. I never touched her."

Clara and Loretta hovered in their bedroom. Then Loretta looked at her and said, "You go and tell her, Clara. You tell her. She'll believe you."

Loud wailing cries erupted from Clara's belly. For a moment, she wondered where the wails were coming from only to realize that it was her pain, spilling out for all the world to hear. The wails were like those of a wounded wolf, howling in the night. She and her sister held each other and cried together, not caring who was watching or what time it was. They only knew that the tears wouldn't stop. They held each other for the first time in a long time and cried. Each girl cried for her sister. Each girl cried for herself. Finally, the tears subsided a little and Loretta and Clara looked at each other. Clara looked out in the driveway and saw that her father's car was still there. She was surprised that their parents never came out to see what all the crying was about. She looked around at the neighbors' houses and saw some of them standing on their porches. Others were peeking from behind their curtains. She glanced at her mother's house. She knew that she couldn't go back in there. "Loretta, do you want to come over to my house?"

Loretta nodded.

They helped each other up and walked over to Clara's BMW. Loretta opened the door on the passenger's side and got in. Clara opened the driver's side door. She stopped and took one last look at her mother's house. With slumped shoulders she got into her car and drove away.

The Edge

Clara woke up the next morning with a splitting headache. She stumbled out of bed and headed to the bathroom holding her head. As she opened the medicine cabinet she caught a glimpse of herself and stepped back in shock. Then she moved forward to take a closer look. Her hair looked like she'd been in a fight. Her eyes were red and puffy from crying through the night. Dried tears streaked her cheeks and her lips were dry and cracked. She looked horrible, but she felt worse.

Clara opened the cabinet again and reached for the extra strength aspirin. She shook out three of the pills and popped them into her mouth while she grabbed a paper cup to get some water to wash them down. She looked at her watch. Eight o'clock. She should be on her way to the Center by now. Her first appointment was at 8:30. But going to the Center was the last thing on Clara's mind.

She didn't think that she could ever go back there. Yesterday her whole world had come crashing in on her. How could she sit in her office and listen to the problems of these women when everything in her was hurting? Help someone? She could help no one in the condition that she was in. How could this have happened to her? How could her father, the man that she had adored when she was a little girl, have done this to them? How could he have done this to her?

Clara grabbed her head as the unanswered questions pushed through her brain, forcing her to try to cope with this whole ordeal that she had blocked out of her memory for so long. She knew that she needed to find a way to get to the Center, but she couldn't.

Clara stumbled back into her bedroom like a drunken woman. She picked up the phone and called her office. Sandra would be there by now. Clara loved the fact that Sandra came in bright and early each morning, often staying as late as Clara needed her to. Clara also appreciated the fact that Sandra never dumped any of her problems on her. She knew that the girl had problems, because she sometimes got this really sad look in her eyes, but she never said anything and that suited Clara just fine.

"Women's Crisis Center." Sandra answered the phone.

"Hi Sandra. It's me. Clara." Clara was not at all surprised that she sounded as bad as she looked.

"Clara, you sound horrible. What's wrong?"

"I'm not feeling too good. I won't be in today. Please ask the other counselors to cover for me today....and tomorrow."

"Okay, I'll do that. You take care of yourself. Okay?" Sandra didn't sound too sure that Clara would.

"Yeah. Thanks." Clara hung up the phone. She sank onto the bed and pulled the covers over her. She pulled her legs up and held onto them tightly. She lay curled up like this, thinking. What was she going to do now? Maybe she could just kill herself. Maybe if she just took all of the pills that she had in the house, she could just die. She felt like dying. Her life was over anyway. If she had a gun, she could just shoot herself. "No, that's crazy," she told herself as she sat up. She didn't want to die. She just wanted this whole thing to be over. She needed someone to talk to. She needed help. She tried to think of a friend that she could call. But she couldn't tell anyone about this. She was too embarrassed. What was she going to do?

Just then she thought about Justine. She could go and see Justine. She would listen. She would know what to do. Clara picked up the phone and dialed the number to the Private Counseling Center. While she waited for the receptionist to pick up, she prayed that Justine could see her today.

....

Clara sat in the parking lot drinking her coffee. It was 10:00 and Justine couldn't see her until eleven. Clara had been sitting here for almost an hour. She had gotten dressed and left the house as soon as they told her that she could come in at eleven. After stopping for coffee, she parked in the parking lot and waited. She had to wait. She was scared that if she didn't, the voices in her head would win. The voices were telling her to throw in the towel. That life wasn't worth living. That she should just go ahead and end it now. But somehow, Clara knew that the voices were trying to fool her. She knew that this could not be the end of her life. That's why she had to wait for Justine right here.

She had left the house this morning before her sister got up. They had stayed up most of the night, crying their hearts out and talking about what had happened when they were just little girls. Her father had definitely raped her sister, and Clara suspected that he had messed with her too. Only she couldn't remember. Her sister didn't remember their father doing anything to Clara. They had talked for hours, trying to dredge up the painful memories so that they could put them behind them. Clara had apologized to her sister for not helping her to get away from their father. She had also begged for her sister's forgiveness for not telling their mother what had really happened.

Loretta had told Clara that it wasn't her fault, that she was just a little girl. Only ten years old. Although her sister forgave her, Clara still felt guilty for not speaking up back then. Things would probably have been different if she had told her mother that she saw her father take her sister out of their bed one night. Her sister didn't come back to bed that night. After that, her father would simply tell her sister to go to his room instead of theirs when it was time to go to bed. Their mother was working through the night and she never knew until Loretta told her.

That's when her mother and father had that big fight and he left the house forever. For a long time after that, Clara wished she had told her mother. Maybe her mother wouldn't have been so mad at her sister. Maybe her mother would have been able to go on with her life. Maybe things would have been better for Loretta. But Clara never did tell and eventually, she just blocked it out of her memory.

Clara buried her face in her hands. How could this have happened? Why did her life have to be like this? The endless questions flowed through her head again. She looked at her watch. Ten fifteen. She opened the car door and headed inside. Perhaps Justine could see her a little earlier. She needed help and she needed help now. As she walked into the Private Counseling Center, she remembered the picture that was hanging in Justine's room. Justine had called him the Savior. Clara wondered was he supposed to be God, or Jesus or something. She had never heard anyone refer to God as the Savior before.

Clara walked over to the desk. "I have an 11:00 appointment with Justine," she told the girl. "I'm a little early. Do you think she can see me now?" Clara's tone was pleading.

"I'll check," the girl said as she picked up the phone and pushed some buttons.

Clara stood there holding her breath, waiting to see what the girl would say.

"Okay. Come on in." She got up and walked over and opened the door for Clara to come in.

Clara smiled as she walked past the girl and headed for the room where she usually met with Justine. At the door, she stopped and looked back at the girl who nodded for her to go on in. Clara turned the knob and opened the door. When she entered the room, Justine was kneeling at the fireplace with her head bowed. Clara walked in and sat down on the sofa.

"Father, I thank you for this meeting that I am now going to have with Clara. Father, I ask that you help me to help her according to your will. I ask that you will enlighten us both and show us what you will have us to see. Father, I thank you for healing Clara. I continue to give you all of the glory and the honor and the praise. In Jesus' name I pray. Amen."

Clara was surprised that Justine was kneeling there praying for her. She had never heard anyone pray for her like that before. She felt a little uncomfortable. Justine sat on the floor in front of the fireplace. When she looked up, Clara thought to herself how beautiful she looked. How peaceful. Clara wished that she had some of that peace right now.

"Clara, you look like you're having a hard time. What's going on?"

Justine's voice was so concerned that Clara started crying.

"Clara, don't cry. Why don't you tell me what's going on?"

Clara took a tissue out of her purse and wiped the tears from her eyes. "Justine, my life is over." Clara crumpled the tissue in her hand. "I took my mother home from the hospital yesterday." She tried to talk

153

through the tears that wouldn't stop. "As we pulled up to the house, I saw a car that I didn't recognize."

Justine just nodded her head.

"When we went into the house, my sister Loretta was in there drunk, and my father was there waiting for my mother to come home."

"How did you feel about that?"

"Horrible," Clara blurted out without thinking. "I mean, I probably should have been glad to see him, but I hate him. You know what Justine?"

"What?"

"When I saw him, I wanted to throw up. I wanted to spit in his face."

Justine got up and walked over to the couch where Clara was sitting. "Clara. What happened next?" She sat down next to Clara.

"Well, my sister told him that she hated him and my mother was blushing like a schoolgirl because he was there." Clara stopped and looked at her hands. "You know, I can't believe that she still loves him after what he did to us."

"Clara, what did he do? And who is us?"

"That pervert raped my sister. He hurt my mother and he hurt me. We are the women that he was supposed to protect and he messed us all up."

Justine took a moment to take this all in. "Clara, are you sure that this happened?"

Clara nodded her head up and down. "Yes, I'm sure. I had forgotten all about it and my sister kept yelling at me that I knew what had happened. She kept screaming at me that I remembered what had happened and then I remembered." Clara wrung her hands. "He did it and my sister told my mother." Clara's eyes met Justine's. She had stopped weeping, but the tears were still flowing down her cheeks. "That bastard told my mother that my sister was lying. My sister begged me to tell them that she was telling the truth...but....I was too scared. I was scared that my mother and my father would be mad at me too...so I didn't say anything...all of these years, I just kept going on with my life while my sister was throwing her life away...and I never said a word...I feel horrible...." Clara covered her face with her hands.

"Clara, you were what, nine, ten years old?" Justine asked her. "Tell me. What were you supposed to do?" She leaned close to Clara and said. "You were a little girl in a grown up world. There is no way that you should have been exposed to such awful stuff. None of this was your fault. Your father is a sick man and you can't blame yourself for that." She pulled Clara's hands from in front of her face. "I have to ask you a question."

Clara just looked at her dazed.

"Did your father rape you too?" Justine asked her.

Clara shook her head. "No. I know for sure that he didn't rape me," she answered Justine. "But I remember that he used to come into our room and sit on my bed. He would stroke my hair and sometimes he would lay down next to me." Clara shook her head again. She wished she had a drink. "He touched me. But he never had sex with me. I remember everything now. He didn't rape me, but I still feel so dirty."

155

Justine took a deep breath. "It's good that he didn't rape you, Clara, but he was wrong for touching you. Clara, as awful as this all is it had to come out." She told Clara. "Now we have to try to get you healed."

Clara nodded her head.

"Clara, you're a psychologist. You do know that one out of four girls is molested by a family member or someone close to the family, don't you?"

Clara nodded her head.

"It's never the child's fault, but the child suffers terribly as a result of the abuse."

Clara just looked at Justine. She knew this but somehow she felt it didn't apply to her.

"Clara, you and your sister did nothing wrong. Your father was the one who was wrong."

Clara looked at her hands. Could Justine be telling her the truth?

"Clara, how do you feel right now?"

"Like dying."

Justine nodded her head. "I thought so." She got up and walked over to the fireplace. She picked up a book from the mantle and came back over to Clara. "Clara, you know that I prayed for you today."

Clara nodded her head.

Justine went on.

"Clara, this is actually a Christian Counseling Center. We are faith based and we do a lot of praying." Justine was turning the pages of the book. Clara realized that it was a bible. "Here everyone believes in God, and we have all accepted Him into our lives. This," She closed the bible and patted the cover, "is our instruction manual for life."

Clara peered at Justine. What was she talking about? Was she actually saying that they were mixing psychology with God? That was crazy. Clara had never heard of anything like this in all of her years of counseling.

"Clara, so often we try to do things on our own, when the fact is that we can do nothing without God," Justine told her. "I have another testimony for you. When my partner and I opened this center, it was just like the one downtown where you work." She sat down next to Clara again as she went on. "We had these big ideas of helping people with our fancy books and the knowledge that we had gained in college about people," Justine said. "The first couple of years were really tough. People came in and out of here and it was like a revolving door. They brought the problems in and they took them back out with them, just like you were telling me earlier." She frowned at the memory. "We were making a difference for some people. Then one day one of our clients committed suicide and we realized we needed to do more."

"Suicide?"

"Yes, suicide. Took a gun and shot herself in the head. Killed instantly. It was at her funeral that we both first heard about the Savior." She waved at the painting on the wall. "Then, a friend invited us to her church shortly after that. My partner and I both accepted God into our lives and after a few months of the teachings at this church, we decided that we would counsel people God's way." She stopped and looked at Clara who was watching her closely. "Now we pray for all of our clients. We pray for your healing and we pray for God to save your souls."

Clara sat up and rubbed her hands over her knees. "I used to go to church," she said. "When I was a little girl, my mother dressed us up and took us to church on Easter."

Justine nodded at her. "I know. That was my story too. My mother and father took us to church every year at Easter, but I knew nothing about God."

"Well, God won't want me." Clara couldn't believe that God would want anything to do with her. "I need to get my life together first."

Justine shook her head. "No, that's where you're wrong. God wants you and he wants you just the way you are. As a mater of fact, he loves you just the way you are. If you will just repent of your sins and accept him into your life, he will take it from there."

Clara couldn't believe this. Here she was in a counseling center and the counselor was telling her that God loved her. How could he? How could anyone love her as messed up as she was? "Really? God loves me? Just like this?" She looked down at herself and back up at Justine again.

"Yes Clara. That's right. If you want to, I will help you to pray for God to come into your life."

Clara thought about what Justine had said for a moment. Then she nodded, "yes, I would like that." She felt a ray of hope. "I need God in my life."

Justine reached for Clara's hands. Then they began to pray.

Voices From The Past

When Clara walked out of the center, the sun was shining and everything looked brighter. She looked at her watch. She couldn't believe that she had been in there with Justine for three hours. After they had prayed, Justine had gotten down to the business of helping Clara to begin to cope with the voices from her past.

Justine had left the room to get some cookies and herbal tea and when she returned Clara started talking. Clara talked and talked and talked. She had never talked so much. The more she talked about her life, the more she remembered. It was no wonder that she was having so many problems in her life. She had suppressed so many of the events from her childhood that she was just a fragment of a person. As she was unveiling these things, she realized that her childhood had not been a happy time at all. Somehow, she had forgotten all of the ugly things and she held on to the few good things that had happened in her childhood. As a result, she had been living her life as a crippled, fragmented individual, using alcohol as a crutch and to fill in the holes. She had been missing a lot of pieces, the pieces that were needed to make her a whole person.

Justine explained to her how important it was to face all of the issues that she had buried in her heart. She convinced Clara to not only remember but to talk about some of the things that had happened.

So Clara did. She talked about her parents drinking, the beatings that she and her sister got, the molestation, the accusations from her mother as they were growing up, the shame, the guilt, the anger, the resentment, and the sense of abandonment that she had felt for most of her life. Clara shed enough tears to fill an ocean during the session. But as she was walking to her car, she felt good. She felt cleansed, and for the first time in her life, she felt whole. Although she was very sad because of what had happened during her childhood, she finally knew who she really was. She felt a power that she had not felt going into the Center. She remembered feeling twinges of what she was feeling now when she was at the hospital and at the Crisis Center over the past couple of days. But those twinges were nothing compared to the surge of power that was flowing through her body right now. Clara knew that she could take on the world and still come out on top.

She slid into the seat of her car and smiled as she turned the key in the ignition. She moved out into traffic and drove towards her house. She had to get home to her sister. They had some more talking to do. Clara wanted to share with her what had happened to her today and then she needed to find

Jason. She had to talk to Jason and let him know that she was going to be okay.

Clara felt a little nervous as she thought about Jason. She had not seen or talked to him since that morning when he came over and found Jeff naked in her kitchen. She knew that he was still mad at her. Maybe she wouldn't call him. Maybe she should just leave him alone. Clara shook her head and made up her mind to call him. She was no longer going to listen to those voices in her head. The days of being controlled by the voices of the past were over.

Today was the first day of the rest of her life. Yes, indeed. Today was a new day and Clara felt like a new woman. She had gotten another chance at life today and she was going to live life to the fullest. From now on, she was going to enjoy life.

....

"Loretta," Clara called as she walked into her house. "Loretta, are you here?" She walked up the stairs and checked the bedrooms and the bathroom. "Loretta," she called again as she went back down to the kitchen. Her heart sank when she saw the empty liquor bottle on the kitchen table next to an ashtray with what looked like marijuana butts in it. Her sister had finished almost a fifth of liquor and from the looks of things she was getting high again. Loretta had been clean for two years. When did she start messing with this stuff again? Clara picked up the phone and dialed her mother's number.

"Hello." Her mother's voice crackled through the receiver.

"Mom, it's me."

"Clara, where are you? How dare you just walk out of here yesterday?" Her mother spoke in the tone that had always scared Clara in the past.

But Clara wasn't feeling scared now. "Mom, have you seen Loretta?" She ignored her mother's question.

"Yeah, she was just here....drunk or high or both."

Her mother's sarcasm pierced Clara's heart.

"Where is she now? Did she say where she was going?"

"Humph. You know better than that. Once that girl starts messing with that stuff, there's no telling where she is or when she'll be back."

"Mom, is Daddy still there?"

"No. You two ran him off again."

"Listen, Mom. I don't want to hurt you, but Loretta and I did not run Daddy off." She took a deep breath. "Mom, Loretta was telling the truth all of those years ago." Clara felt the weight lifting from her shoulders. "She wasn't lying. I knew and I was too scared to say anything. Mom, are you still there?"

"Clara, I can see that your sister has gotten to you now. You know that your father would never do anything to hurt either one of you."

Clara could hear the tears in her mother's voice.

"I don't know why you girls want to hurt me and your father, but I wish you would stop."

Clara had to hang up. Her mother was in denial. She and Justine had talked about that.

"Listen, Mom, I have to go now. If you hear from Loretta, tell her to call me. Okay?" Clara paused. "And Mom, tell her that I love her. Okay?"

"Okay. I'll tell her. Although, I don't think it's going to make much difference."

"Mom, are you feeling okay?" Clara remembered to ask.

"Yeah, I feel good. What a weird thing to happen to me. I can't even tell that something was wrong with my heart."

Clara thought about what God had done for her mother. She silently prayed that her mother would change her ways. "Good, Momma. I'm glad to hear you're okay. Well, I have to go. Don't forget what I said to tell Loretta, and Momma." Clara waited for her mother to answer her.

"What?"

"Momma, I love you too. And please, no drinking okay?"

"Who's the mother around here? In case you've forgotten, I'm the mother and I can handle my liquor."

Clara sighed. Just as she thought, her mother was drinking already. The incident with her heart had not even scared her enough to make her stop drinking for a little while. She and her father had probably gotten drunk yesterday. "Okay, Mom. I'll call you tomorrow."

"Okay. Bye."

Clara hung up the phone and walked into the living room. She sat on the sofa and reached for the remote control. She noticed that there was another bottle of liquor on the coffee table. She thought that it would be nice to have a drink. But she shook her head, got up, grabbed the bottle and ran to pour it out in the kitchen sink. No. She would not give in to the voices from the past. She didn't need liquor, and she didn't need to drown out the pain anymore. She had faced the pain and she had survived after all. She opened the cabinet where she kept her liquor and began to pour it all out. She opened bottles and poured out wine and liquor until it was all gone. No more excuses, she was ready to face life now.

....

Clara went back into the living room and sat down on the couch. She looked around and realized that she really did have a nice place. Only one thing was missing and that was her man.

Clara picked up the phone and dialed Jason's number. She needed to talk to him. She had to tell him what had happened that morning. She wanted to beg him to forgive her and to tell him that she loved him. She held her breath as the phone rang once, than twice. Finally, it was picked up on the third ring.

"Hello," a woman's voice answered.

Clara started to hang up, but decided to go ahead and ask for Jason. "Hello, is Jason there?"

"No, may I ask who's calling?"

"Oh. This is Clara. I wanted to see how he was doing."

"Oh. Well he's not here right now. Can I have him call you?"

"No, that's okay. Just tell that I called to say hello. As matter of fact, that's okay. Please, don't even tell him that I called."

"Okay."

Clara hung up the phone and sat there staring at the TV. She wondered if that was Monica who answered the phone. And if it was, what was she doing at Jason's house when he wasn't home. Was she living there now? Clara felt like the bottom was dropping out of her stomach. Had she lost Jason forever? It certainly looked like it. Monica was hanging on pretty tightly. "Well, who wouldn't?" Clara scolded herself. "You had a chance to have him, and you blew it." Now she had to face the fact that she was not getting Jason back. She had not been ready to give him what he needed, and he had found it with another woman. She had to live with that. She would just go on with her life. Maybe one day she would meet someone else. But she didn't want someone else. She wanted Jason. She loved him and she needed him in her life. She thought that maybe they could be friends, but she knew that she couldn't live with that. She decided to just leave him alone. She wouldn't call him again. That was it. She would just let him go on with his life. After all, he deserved to be happy, with or without her. As she thought about living her life without Jason, the phone rang. She jumped at the sudden interruption.

"Hello."

"Hi Clara."

Clara swooned at the sound of Jason's voice.

"Jason. Hi."

"Clara, I walked in as Monica was hanging up with you. Is everything okay? Are you alright?"

"Yes." Clara nodded her head. "I'm fine. Everything's fine. I was just calling to say hi and when Monica answered the phone, I didn't feel that it was right for you to call me back. So I...."

"So you told her not to even tell me that you called." Jason finished for her.

"Yes. I really didn't see the need for you to call me back."

"There you go again. It's always about what Clara wants, isn't it? I come over there and there is some man standing in your kitchen with nothing but a towel on and you have the nerve to get upset because Monica answered my phone."

Clara searched for a way to stop him. She didn't want to argue with him. She had just wanted to hear his voice. "Listen, Jason. I didn't call to argue with you. I just wanted to hear your voice." She took a deep breath and went on. "Look, I've been through a lot since I last saw you and I just needed to hear a friendly voice." She was crying. God, she didn't want to cry. Not now while she was talking to Jason.

"Clara, I asked you if you were okay."

"And I am."

"Well, why don't I come over there and sit with you for a little while? We could just sit and talk if you like."

Clara wanted that. She wanted him to come more than anything in the world, but what about Monica? She was there with Jason now. How could he just leave his woman and come over to her house? And what if she didn't want him to leave once he got there, but he had to leave because he had to go home to Monica? No, Clara knew that she couldn't stand that. She would not share Jason with Monica. She would not be the other woman. She would never be able to live like that.

"Clara? Clara, are you still there?"

"Sorry. I was just thinking about if you should come over here and I don't think that's such a good idea." There. She had said it.

"Clara, you sound like you're going through something. Why don't you let me go through it with you?"

"Because I need to do this alone. I need to go through this and I need to do it by myself. Okay?" She hoped that he wouldn't take no for an answer. Why couldn't he just hang up the phone and come over to be with her?

"Okay, Clara. Have it your way. As usual." Jason's tone was angry again. "I hope everything works out for you. You always have to be so strong and so much in control." He went on, "Maybe for once, you could learn to lean on someone. Everybody needs someone, Clara. Everybody. Even you."

"I know, Jason. And you're right. I do need someone. But I can't let you come over here right now."

Jason sighed and said, "Okay. Listen, I have to go. I'll talk to you. Okay?"

"Okay." Clara hung up the phone. She knew full well that she would probably never talk to him again. She couldn't. He had already replaced her and it hurt too much to even talk to him. Clara's heart was broken. But she was going to be okay. She was going to get over this. After all, she had gone through worse things in her life and survived. She looked at her watch. It was four thirty. She needed to get out of this house. She would take a ride. Perhaps see the new movie about the guy who had these imaginary people following him around, talking to him all the time. Yeah, that's what she'd do. It would help her to take her mind off Jason and Monica and Loretta and her mother and father. It would help her to relax a little. She grabbed her keys and headed for the door.

Love Is...

She drove to the movie theater and was happy to see that the movie she wanted to see was going to start in ten minutes.

She stood in line behind a guy and a girl. The couple was obviously arguing. The girl was telling the guy that she wanted to see one movie and he was insisting that they see the one he wanted to see.

"Why can't we ever see what I want to see?" the girl pouted.

"Because it was my idea to see a movie and I'm paying. So I should pick the movie."

What a jerk. Clara thought as she eavesdropped on their conversation.

The girl looked unhappy. She folded her arms in front of her and turned away.

"Listen. If you're going to act like a spoiled brat, then we can just get out of here now." The guy walked away from the line, leaving his girlfriend standing there. "Come on. Let's go."

The girl just stood there, looking straight ahead.

"Come on. What are you doing? I said let's go." The guy sounded angry now.

The girl looked at him for a moment. Then she said, "I want to see the movie I picked."

"Are you deaf?" The guy was yelling now. "I am not putting up with your stupid moods tonight. I said let's go." He grabbed her arm and yanked her out of the line.

Clara took a step forward. She wanted to stop the guy. She wanted to tell the girl that she didn't have to take that from this jerk, but she stood still, not saying a word.

"Stop," the girl squealed in pain. "You're hurting me."

Clara's heart went out to this girl. She was too young to even be out on a date with him. She could not have been more than fifteen. The guy looked to be about twenty. He still had his fingers clamped around the girl's arm, not caring who was watching them.

"Come on, we're getting out of here."

The girl dug in her heels to prevent him from dragging her out the door.

"No. Stop it! I told you. You're hurting me!"

"Listen, if you don't come on, I'm really going to hurt you."

That was it for Clara. She couldn't hold it in anymore. "Hey you," she called out to the guy. When he looked at her, she took a deep breath and went on. "What do you think you're doing?" Clara demanded of him. "Let her go."

"Listen lady. I don't know what your problem is, but this is my girl. I can do what I like to her."

"No, you can't." Clara was very angry now. She tried to keep her voice calm. "Now you will let her go and you'll let her go now." By this time, everyone in line was paying attention to the scene that was being played out in the lobby.

"Lady, you're nuts. Here, you can have her. She's nothing but trash anyway." He flung the girl's arm towards Clara so hard that the girl went stumbling into Clara's arms.

Clara caught her and steadied her. They both looked up in time to see the guy walking out of the door.

Tears were streaming down the girls cheeks.

"Why are you crying?"

"He's leaving me. How am I going to get home?" The girl looked scared.

Clara wondered where her parents were. "I could take you home. Do your parents know that you were with that jerk?"

The girl's eyes filled with fear as she shook her head from side to side. "No. My parents don't know anything about him."

Clara had guessed as much.

"My parents are so busy with their careers and their high class friends that they don't even know if I'm dead or alive."

"Now, I think you're stretching the truth a little there." Clara smiled at the girl. She knew that feeling. It was the same feeling that she had gotten year after year while her parents spent their time partying, entertaining their friends, drinking and fighting. Suddenly she had an idea. "Listen, I'll give you a ride home but since we're here, why don't we go on in to see the movie you picked? I hear it's a great movie and I was on my way to see it myself. How about it? Do you want to go on in?"

The girl hesitated.

"My treat," Clara added.

The girl nodded her head. "Okay."

"Great!" Clara was glad to have some company. "Come on. Let's go and get our tickets. Oh. My name is Clara. What's yours?"

"Lisa."

"Hi Lisa, I'm glad to meet you." Clara paid for the tickets. They got some popcorn, candy, and soda and headed into the theater. Lisa was such a sweet girl. Clara wondered how her parents could let their little girl run around town unsupervised. There were a lot of sick people out there and it looked like Lisa had hooked up with one of them. Clara wondered if he would come back in. She vowed not to let Lisa leave with him. She could see that he had some very bad tendencies. She made a mental note to talk to Lisa about him after the movie.

Clara was glad that Lisa's boyfriend was not outside the theater when they came out after the movie. She noticed that Lisa was looking around for him and seemed to be disappointed when she didn't see him. Clara felt sorry for this pretty young girl. How could her parents be so caught up in their careers that they couldn't see that their little girl was crying out for attention? "Lisa, are you ready to go home?"

Lisa nodded her head.

"My car is over there." They walked over and got into Clara's car. As Clara turned the key in the ignition and started to pull out of the parking lot, she noticed that Lisa was still looking around. "Lisa, why are you looking for him?"

Lisa looked as if she had been caught with her hand in the cookie jar. "I was just wondering if he was still here. He has always come back for me before."

Clara couldn't believe this. "You mean to tell me that he's left you before?"

Lisa nodded her head again. "Only for a couple of hours or so. He's never left me and not come back. He only does it to teach me not to talk back to him."

"Lisa, do you think it's okay for him to just take off and leave you places?"

"Like I said, he always comes back for me."

Clara couldn't believe that this young girl was defending that punk. "Lisa, why do you hang out with someone who treats you like he does?"

Lisa shrugged her shoulders. "Oh, it's not too bad. Besides, he loves me."

That was it. Clara knew that the only reason that this pretty young girl put up with this abusive behavior from her boyfriend was because she thought he loved her. She had the signs of a young girl who was looking for love in all the wrong places. Her daddy probably never paid any attention to her and from the sounds of things, neither did her mother. Clara took a deep breath.

"Lisa, that's not love. Love is when a man opens doors for you. He'll treat you like you're glass, like you might break. He'll speak gently to you for fear that he'll hurt your feelings." Clara smiled as she described what love was like. "Love is when your heart pounds at the sound of his name, not with fear but anticipation. A man that loves you will never call you names. He'll never leave you unprotected. Love is when a man would give you the world if he had it to give." Clara paused. "When a man loves you, he'll be gentle and kind and thoughtful...opening doors and pulling out chairs...telling you that you're beautiful and how much he loves you..." Tears streamed down Clara's face as she talked.

"Are you okay, Ms. Clara?"

Clara wiped her tears and nodded her head. "Yes, Lisa. I'm okay. It's just that I had a very special love like the one I'm telling you about and I blew it."

"How?"

"I was too stupid to realize what real love was. By the time I found out, it was too late. He already had another girlfriend."

"Oh, no!"

Clara smiled through her tears at the childlike exclamation. She could tell that Lisa felt really bad about what had happened to her. "Listen. You are a really sweet, pretty, young lady. Don't let any boy treat you like dirt. You deserve better than that. If a boy doesn't treat you like a queen, you don't need him." Clara took a tissue out of the glove department and dried her tears. "Lisa, do you understand what I'm saying to you?"

"Yes, I understand." Lisa nodded as she sat looking out of the window on the passenger side.

Clara kept quiet to allow the girl to think about what she had said. After a few minutes, they turned into Lisa's street. It had not been hard to find since she lived only a few blocks from Clara.

As she pulled up to the house that Lisa pointed out to her, she handed Lisa her card. "Here is my card. Both my home and work numbers are on it."

Lisa took the card and stuck it into her pocket.

"You can call me anytime. If you want to talk, call me. Okay?"

"Okay." Lisa opened the car door.

Clara noticed that most of the lights were on in the house. Well, at least the girl's parents were home.

"Bye, Ms. Clara. Thanks." Lisa said as she got out of the car.

"Bye, Lisa. Remember what I said. You're a princess, growing up to be a queen and you should be treated like one. Okay?"

"Okay."

"Bye Lisa." Clara watched Lisa close the car door and head up the walk. Clara didn't know if she was imagining things or not, but it looked like Lisa had an extra bounce in her step as she walked up the walkway to her home with her head held high. Clara smiled as she started the car and headed home.

Before It's Too Late

When Clara walked into her house the phone was ringing. She rushed over and picked it up, wondering who could be calling her at this hour.

"Hello." She was out of breath from running to the phone.

"Clara?"

"Francine? Is everything okay?"

"Clara. I needed someone to talk to. I've been calling you all night."

"What's wrong?"

"Clara. My mother...died today."

"Oh, no. Francine, I'm so sorry."

"Clara, she died with me mad at her. I never even got the chance to say goodbye." Francine's sobs tore into Clara. What could she possibly say to her friend who had spent most of her life mad at her mother? She remembered the last conversation she had with Francine.

"Francine, do you need me to come over there?"

"No...I need to be by myself."

"Okay. But I'll call you tomorrow to see if you need anything."

"Clara. I wish I had listened to you. You tried to tell me to talk to my mother. I feel so bad. I never went over there to talk to her. I never forgave her."

Clara could only imagine the pain that Francine was feeling. She wished she had the words to make her feel better. But at times like this, there were no words. "Francine, your mother is resting in peace now. I'm sure she knew that you loved her."

"Do you really think so, Clara? Do you think she knew that I really didn't hate her?"

"Yes I think she knew. Francine, your mother was proud of you. She regretted the way she treated you when you were a kid, but she loved you. She told me once that she wished things could be different between the two of you. She really did care about you."

"You never told me she told you that."

"That's because you were having such a hard time in your relationship with her." Clara didn't want to mention that she had tried and that her friend had refused to listen. "Take it from me. Your mother really loved you."

Francine sniffled. "Thanks Clara. That helps. I really miss my mother."

"I know. I'm sorry."

"Thanks. I have to go. Someone's trying to call on the other line. This phone won't stop ringing."

"Okay. I'll call you tomorrow."

"Okay Clara, and thanks again."

Clara hung up the phone and sank into a kitchen chair. What a shame. Francine had stayed mad at her mother for so long and now her mother was dead. Clara felt sorry for her friend. She picked up her bag and headed up the stairs. She needed to get some rest. Maybe tomorrow would be a better day.

Back To Work

The next morning, Clara got up early and headed to the office. As she walked into the office, she was surprised to see Sandra sitting at her desk crying. She quickly walked over to her. "Sandra, what's the matter?"

Sandra reached for a tissue to dry her eyes. "I don't know what to do."

Clara looked around to see if anyone else was in the office. She sighed with relief when she noticed that she and Sandra were the only ones there. She knew that Sandra was a very private person and would never want anyone in the office to know her business. She always said that they all had enough problems of their own. She hated the fact that women came in here and told all of their business. She felt that her private business was just that and that whatever she was going through was nobody's business.

Clara had laughed when she first heard that, but she often found herself using the very same phrase with Jason, telling him that her business was nobody's business. She was glad that she had found out that this was not true. Since meeting Justine, she realized that the stuff that hurt to the core needed to be told to someone. It helped to talk to someone before the issues that were considered to be nobody's business made you sick, or worse, sent you to an early grave.

"Sandra, you need to talk about this. What is it?" Clara insisted.

"My baby's pregnant." Sandra sighed. She seemed relieved to get that out.

"Are you sure? She's only...."

"Fourteen," Sandra finished for her. "What did I do wrong? I sent her to the best schools. I haven't had a date in years. I spent all of my free time with her. How could this have happened?"

Clara searched for words that would help. What could she say to this mother who had sacrificed her whole life for her young daughter just so the girl could have a better chance at life than she did? The girl was only fourteen years old. She was going to be a mother at fifteen? Clara put her arm around Sandra who turned and wept in Clara's arms. Clara just stood there, patting Sandra on the back.

"It's going to be okay. No matter what happens, you must let your daughter know that you still love her."

"I'm...so...dis...appointed with her." Sandra could barely speak. "I am...so...mad at her. I could kill her." She pushed away from Clara and wiped her face with the back of her hand. "I've spent my whole life sacrificing for that child so she could have better than I did. She's an A student. She had her entire life ahead of her. Why would she sneak around and have sex? I didn't even know that she was interested in boys. No one has ever called the house." Sandra rambled on as though she was searching for answers.

"When did she see him?"

"After school and when I went to the gym for two hours on Saturday. The punk was sneaking over to my house, laying up with my little girl." Sandra sounded like smoke should have been coming out of her ears. "The worst part about it is he's three years older than she is. If he was eighteen, I'd put him in jail for statutory rape." She paced the small area in front of her desk. "And to top it off, he wants to marry my daughter. That would really ruin her life. He hasn't even finished high school. He dropped out and works in his father's garage. What sort of life could he offer my daughter?"

Clara let Sandra get it all out without interrupting her. Then she asked, "Sandra, what does your daughter want to do?"

"Humph, she wants to marry the bum. Can you imagine that?" Sandra snorted. "Two high school dropouts and a baby. What would they do? Where would they live?"

"Well, things have a way of working out. I'm not going to try to give you the standard psychological answers, but you'll probably be amazed at how things work out in the end. You may not want to hear this, but if those kids want to get married, you might want to consider letting them. Your other option is to let her have the baby and help her to take care of it while she finishes school."

"I spent my whole life raising that girl. I don't want to raise grandbabies too. I think she should have an abortion. But I can't make her."

Clara shook her head. She was relieved that Sandra's daughter didn't want an abortion. She was totally against abortion. "No, you can't make her. Besides, she'll just get pregnant again. Don't you know that when young girls are forced to have abortions, they get pregnant again almost right away to replace the baby that they got rid of?"

Sitting on the edge of her desk, Sandra shook her head. "No, I didn't know that. Why in the world would they do that?"

"It's a psychological thing." Clara sat down in the chair next to Sandra's desk. "Most of them have such great feelings of guilt and emptiness, that it becomes a mission for them to get pregnant again."

Sandra stood up and walked back around the desk. She dropped back into her chair and grabbed another tissue from the box. "What am I going to do? What will my friends think?"

"Don't worry about what people will think or say. You just keep on loving your little girl and be there to support her. Take it from me. That's the most important thing. Don't lose the love of your little girl because she made a mistake."

"Okay." Sandra's wiped her eyes again. "I do love my baby. No matter what."

"Good. Now, why don't you go home and spend the day with her. Have a talk with her and let her know you're in her corner. Go on. You can have the day off with pay."

Sandra stood up and picked up her bag. "Thanks, Clara." She headed for the door. As if thinking about it further, she stopped and turned around to look at Clara. "Really thanks."

"You're welcome," Clara said as she watched her secretary leave.

Clara walked over to her desk and looked down at her appointment book. She saw that Sandra had scheduled all of her regular appointments with the other counselors. She looked over the appointment book and made a note to speak to her colleagues to see if she should take any of the appointments or perhaps just do walk-ins.

As she was checking the book, she heard someone come into the center. She looked up and saw a girl walking towards her with her head down. She shuffled her feet as she walked. She was dressed in a baseball cap with her hair pulled back in a ponytail. She had on glasses and wore a gray jogging suit with sneakers.

"This girl needs a makeover," Clara thought to herself as the girl finally stood in front of her. "May I help you?"

"Yes, I'm here to see you."

Clara recognized the girl's soft, meek voice at once. "Jennifer? Is that you?"

"Yes, I've been waiting for you. I came in yesterday and they tried to make me see someone else." She shook her head from side to side as she adjusted her glasses. "I don't want to see anyone else. I only want to see you. Can I come in?" She glanced in the direction of Clara's office.

"Yes, come in." Clara didn't know if she was ready for this, but she had decided to come in and now she had to deal with Jennifer and perhaps even Jennie. She composed herself as she followed Jennifer into the office and sat in the chair behind her desk. "Have a seat Jennifer." She waved towards the seating area.

Jennifer sat on the sofa and looked down at her lap. "Clara, you have to help me," she said as she looked frantically around the room." Jennie is out of control. I don't think I can stand it anymore."

Clara made a notation on her pad. "What do you mean, out of control?"

"Just that. She refuses to let me sleep with my husband. Instead, she goes around sleeping with every man she meets, and she's still sleeping with him."

"Him? Who's him?"

Jennifer ducked her head down and looked around the office as if someone was watching them. "I promised her that I wouldn't tell anyone, so I can't tell you." She lowered her voice. "But I can't stand for him to touch me anymore." She leaned over towards Clara and whispered. "I wish that I could get rid of Jennie so that I could have some peace."

Clara became alarmed. It was common in split personality disorders for one of the personalities to want to get rid of the other. She remembered from her textbooks that this type of thinking often resulted in suicide because the one would believe that by killing the other personality they could continue to exist. "Jennifer, you and Jennie share the same body. And you should know, anything that you do to her will affect you too."

"I know." Jennifer let her eyes meet Clara's for the first time. "I almost don't care. If I die, then I won't have to live with them anymore."

"Jennifer, who are you talking about?"

"Them." Her voice was flat and cold. "Jennie is a whore. She has all of these men grabbing and feeling all over me and sticking their dirty things in me. I only want to be with my own husband, and she has me cheating on him."

"Oh, so he's your husband?"

"Yeah, I married him and Jennie has never liked him. As a matter of fact, they hate each other. Whenever Jennie is around, she starts fights with him."

Clara was starting to get the picture. Jennifer was the good girl, and Jennie was the bad girl. How common for this disorder. "Why does she do this?"

Jennifer shrugged her shoulders. "I told you. She hates him and she's out of control. She's a slut, and she wants to get him out of the way so that she can sleep around with the others."

"How long has she been acting like this?"

"Since we were fifteen." Jennifer spat out the words. "That's when she gave our virginity to him."

Clara was surprised to see how angry Jennifer was. "Okay, who is him?" she tried again.

Jennifer wrung her hands on her lap.

"I can't help you if you don't tell me about him." Clara was getting impatient. "In order for us to make progress, I need to know everything. Who did she give your virginity to?"

Jennifer continued to wring her hands nervously in her lap. She then put them on the sides of the chair and shifted from side to side. Clara watched with fascination as Jennifer crouched down in her chair and turned her head to the right and then to the left as if listening for something. "Did you hear that?" she whispered.

"No I didn't hear anything," Clara answered as she watched Jennifer closely.

"Shhhhhh." Jennifer put her finger to her lips. "They're looking for me."

"Who? Who's looking for you?" This was getting a little too weird for Clara.

"Jennie and him. They're coming to get me." Jennifer looked petrified.

"Jennifer, wait. No one is here. Jennie might come but I don't understand. Who is him?" Clara was more than a little nervous. Was Jennifer losing her mind?

"You know. They're coming to get me. Don't let them get me." Jennifer got up and crouched behind her chair as if hiding from these unseen guests.

"Okay." Clara searched for the right words to say. She watched Jennifer carefully, wondering what had brought this on. "Jennifer I told you there's no one here."

Jennifer peeked out from behind the chair. "You've got to help me," she said in a very soft voice. "I'm scared."

"You don't have to be scared." Clara tried to keep her voice calm. "Come on out and talk to me." She held out her hand. "They're not here. They can't hurt you."

"Do you promise?" Jennifer sounded like a scared little girl.

"I promise." Was she crazy? How could she make such a promise?

Jennifer came slowly from behind the chair. She sat down and wiped her hands on the front of her sweat suit. "Whew." She smiled at Clara. "That was close."

Clara blinked her eyes in confusion. Was Jennifer schizophrenic? She didn't know where to go from here. Maybe she should just end this session. She had promised herself that she wouldn't deal with these two. Now here she was in the middle of a session that she wasn't sure she could handle. Jennifer had taken this thing to another level. Clara knew that the best thing to do was to just get out of there, but she felt the need to go on. She wanted to help Jennifer. If she sent her away, she might kill herself. Clara remembered what it felt like to want to die. She decided that she would stick it out with Jennifer and get to the bottom of this. "Jennifer, who took your virginity?" She repeated her question from earlier looking straight at Jennifer.

Jennifer looked around the room again.

Clara wondered if she would give a repeat performance of the last scene. She was surprised when Jennifer looked at her and spoke in a clear voice.

"Okay. I'll tell you." She took a deep breath in and then exhaled.

Clara moved closer to the edge of her seat.

"It's my stepfather."

Clara grabbed the arms of her chair as she felt the room tilt. She had the familiar feeling of wanting to throw up. What was the problem with these men? She thought angrily. How could they just mess up a young girl's life and then act like nothing ever happened? Fifteen? Jennifer had been only fifteen. What decent man would sleep with a girl of fifteen? Clara forced herself to go on. "Jennifer, did he rape you?"

Jennifer was shaking her head back and forth, back and forth. "No, Jennie seduced him. She said that he was too much man for my mother." Jennifer went on. "She was always his favorite, always sitting on his lap and kissing him and hugging him. He loved the attention she gave him and every day, he would bring her toys and stuff." Jennifer shifted her weight in the chair again. "Then one night, I woke up in the middle of the night and they were in bed together. I started screaming and Momma came in and saw them and started hollering for him to stop. He jumped up and told Momma that she wasn't woman enough for him and that he had to get it somewhere." Jennifer wept as she told the story.

Clara didn't want to hear anymore. But Jennifer kept talking as Clara sat in her chair wishing that the room would stop spinning.

"Momma kind of went crazy. She went back to their bedroom and got in the bed. That's where she's been ever since. The doctor came over and gave her some sedatives and then some antidepressant pills.

Now all she does is stay in bed and take her pills. She sleeps most of the time and when she wakes up, she takes some more pills to make her sleep again." Jennifer was still crying. Clara was crying. Clara was sure that God was crying too.

"Jennifer. Do you still live in the house with your stepfather?"

"Yes. Jennie won't let me leave. I have to stay there with my husband and pretend that they're not using my body the way that they do. I'm so afraid that my husband will find out. I don't know what to do."

"Jennifer, it's not your fault that your stepfather took your virginity." This whole conversation was much too familiar to Clara. "You were a kid. You didn't seduce him. You didn't ask for it. He bought you things to win you over, and then he manipulated you to make you think that it was all your fault."

Clara knew that she was pushing it, but she was hoping that the truth would set Jennifer free.

"Jennifer, you and Jennie are innocent. Actually, Jennie only came into your life to be the bad guy, to take the blame. That's not fair to her. Neither one of you are to blame. Your mother is sick because she refuses to face the reality that her husband is sleeping with her daughter. She should have protected you from him."

Jennifer was looking at Clara as if she wanted to believe what she was saying.

"Where's Jennie?"

"I'm not letting her out."

Clara could hear the determination in Jennifer's voice.

"I need her to stop this. I need her to stop sleeping with him."

Clara nodded her head. "Okay, that's good. That means that you have more control then Jennie does. You're stronger than she is. You can make her go away for good. Would you like to do that?"

Jennifer nodded without saying a word.

"Good, now you just keep her in there and I'm going to help you get rid of her for good." Clara felt like she was making progress with Jennifer. "The first step is to want to get well. I know that you do because you wouldn't be here if you didn't. The next step is for you to know that whatever happened is not your fault, okay?"

"Okay." Jennifer had stopped crying. "Clara, I need to tell you something." Her voice was stronger.

"What is it, Jennifer?"

"Clara, my stepfather told us that he had two daughters and another wife across town."

Clara's heart dropped. Oh God no. Please, don't let her say it, please.

"My stepfather is your daddy." As Jennie pushed Jennifer aside, her voice taunted Clara. "He's your daddy, Clara. Why did he hurt us? Why did your daddy hurt my family?"

Clara heard herself screaming. "No, no, no. No, God no. It can't be. No!"

Jennie got up and walked over to her. "Your father likes to rape little girls, does he? Well, I'll show him what it's like to have a real woman."

190

Clara shivered at Jennie's menacing tone. "My father...?"

"Don't worry. I'll take care of him." The words sounded like they were from a bad horror movie. "I'll take care of him. Don't you worry about a thing." Jennie stood over Clara. "Oh, and by the way, you and the geek can forget about getting rid of me." She leaned down to look Clara in the eyes. "I'm not the one who's going, she is." She patted Clara on the head and walked out of the door.

Clara's sanity was slipping away. She cried out. "Oh God, please help me. God, please don't let me lose my mind. Help me." Suddenly, she lost consciousness.

What A Price To Pay

Clara woke up in a strange room. She looked around the pretty bedroom and wondered where she was. She tried to sit up but her head was pounding so hard that she fell back against the pillow. Memories of her meeting with Jennifer came crashing back at her. She grabbed her head and let out a loud moan. Within seconds, Justine was standing at her side.

"Clara, you're awake. Are you okay?" Justine sat down and reached for her hands to try to calm her.

"Oh, Justine. Thank God," Clara sighed with relief holding on to Justine's hands. "I'm so glad to see you." She looked around the room again. "Where am I? How did I get here?"

"Wait. Slow down. One question at a time, okay? You're at my house. I came into your office to talk to you about a conference that I wanted you to help me put together and I found you slumped over your desk."

"Yeah. I think I remember losing control." Clara rubbed her forehead.

"You looked like you were unconscious. I was going to take you to the hospital, but then you started talking to me," Justine continued. "You knew who I was and you kept saying help me over and over again. So I decided to bring you to my house."

"How long...?" Clara leaned back against the pillow.

"I've been waiting for you to wake up," Justine interrupted her. "You must have been exhausted. You've been out for hours."

"Oh, my head feels like somebody beat me up," Clara said rubbing her forehead again. "Do you know what happened?"

Justine shook her head. "You kept saying something that sounded like daddy. I couldn't make it out."

"Daddy? Oh no." Clara stopped rubbing her head. "My father. He didn't stop with Loretta and me. He went across town and started living with this lady who had a daughter." As she told Justine the story, she felt like throwing up again. She forced herself to go on through the lump in her throat and through the tears.

"He's been sleeping with the girl for twenty years. How could he do that and get away with it?" Clara asked, confused.

"Oh Clara, I'm sorry." Justine hugged Clara.

Clara continued to weep.

"Look, don't let this destroy you. You can handle this. You have to stay strong. The Center needs you. Your clients need you."

Clara just stared at Justine as if she didn't know who she was.

"Clara, do you want to go to the hospital?"

Clara tried to shake her head, but it hurt too much. "No. Can I just stay here?"

"You can stay here for as long as you like." Justine stood up. "Can I get you anything?"

"No, I just want to lay here and do some thinking if that's okay."

"That's fine." Justine walked over to the door. "Call me if you need me. I'll be in the room next door. Okay?"

"Okay." Clara closed her eyes and tried to shut out the awful truth about her father. What a horrible man he was. How could he do this to her? She thought as the tears continued to flow from her closed lids.

Over the next few hours, Clara drifted in and out of a deep sleep. Justine came in often to check on her and to see if she needed anything. Finally Clara woke up. She was starving and she needed to go to the bathroom. Her legs were so weak that she fell when she tried to get out of the bed.

Justine came running in to see if she was okay. "I guess you're still a little wobbly. Here let me help you." Justine helped her to sit on the edge of the bed.

"Could you help me to the bathroom?"

"Sure. Lean on me." As they walked, Clara started to feel stronger. "I can take it from here."

"I'll just wait out here. Just in case you need me to walk you back."

Clara went into the bathroom and shut the door. She was grateful for a friend like Justine. She couldn't remember anyone taking care of her like this. Except for Jason. He had taken care of her, always concerned about how she was doing or how she was feeling or if there was anything he could do for her. Boy, she was a real fool for letting him get away. Se la vie. She couldn't do anything about that now. Besides, he was probably madly in love with Monica by now.

She just hoped that she would one day find love like that again and not end up with someone like her father. Her head hurt just to think about the man. And he walked around like he wasn't doing anything wrong. Clara wondered how he could even look at himself in the mirror. She wanted to hate him, but she could only remember that hurting people hurt people. At that moment, she knew that she had no choice but to forgive him. She would forgive him because God had forgiven her and she needed to be free from any feelings of bitterness and anger that could come from being unforgiving.

She was feeling better. She wondered what she could do to help Jennifer or Jennie or whatever her name was. She knew that she could not counsel her any longer. It was almost as if she had tried to do Clara in. Clara remembered how Jennifer's personality had left and Jennie's had taken over. Clara was convinced that Jennie had intentionally tried to hurt her. She remembered the pat on the head and shivered. She thought about calling the police. But what could she tell them? She had nothing to report. She had the feeling that something was horribly wrong. What if Jennifer tried to kill herself? Somehow, Clara had to talk to someone about this. She decided to call her friend at Bergen County Psychiatric Counseling Center tomorrow and see if he could help her.

"Clara, are you okay in there?" Justine called through the door.

"Yes, I'm coming out now." Clara came out of the bathroom and walked over to the bed where she lay back against the pillows. She nodded towards the television set in the corner. "Does that television set work?"

"Un-huh," Justine said and picked up the remote from the nightstand. She flicked the television set on and surfed through the channels.

Clara watched as Justine turned the channels, pausing for a minute at each station so that Clara could decide what to watch. She stopped at the news station and was just about to switch the channel when Clara sat up in bed.

"Wait!" she cried out holding up her hand.

Justine pressed the back button to go back to the channel she had just switched from.

Clara sat bolt upright in the bed and pointed at the television screen.

"That's Jennifer!" She stared at the television as Jennifer was being put into an ambulance.

This had to be a really bad dream. There was this guy in handcuffs and someone was on a stretcher.

The newscaster was reporting.

"Local man is arrested for shooting and killing his wife's stepfather. It appears that his wife had been having an affair with her stepfather. The suspect is said to have come home and found them in bed together. In his rage, he grabbed his gun and shot at the couple, fatally wounding his wife's stepfather. The wife is unharmed but seems to be in a daze and unaware of what has happened. When police arrived, she was sitting naked in a corner of the bedroom sucking her thumb. She has been taken to Bergen County Medical Center to be examined by the doctors there. The wife is said to have a twin sister who we have been unable to locate. The couple lived in the house with the wife's mother and stepfather. The wife's mother was found in an upstairs bedroom heavily sedated. Neighbors say that she has not left the house in years. Many said that they did not know that she was still alive. Neighbors also say that they suspected that something strange was going on in the house seen here. More news will be released pending further investigation."

"That's the girl I was telling you about," Clara said still pointing at the television. Then as she realized what the reporter had said she dropped her hand in her lap. "My father's dead. He killed my father."

Justine stood frozen, looking at Clara.

"Jennifer's husband shot and killed my father," Clara repeated. "What a price to pay."

Justine started to pace back and forth. She seemed to be deep in thought. She just kept walking back and forth in front of the television set. Her lips were moving but no words came out.

Clara realized that she was praying. Justine was always praying about something. Perhaps that was the reason she stayed so calm all of the time. Clara was grateful that she had Justine for a friend. She needed her strength right now. She needed a sense of peace. She really needed to know that she was not alone right now.

Without Justine, she would have no one to help her to deal with what had just happened. Jason was with Monica. Loretta was nowhere to be found. Her mother was acting crazy and Sandra had her own problems. Clara thanked God that Justine had come into her office and found her. She could have gone crazy, but it wasn't meant to be. Just then, she realized that she would be okay. She would make it through this. Just then she felt a great sense of peace.

Clara took another look at the facts. Her sister was drunk and on drugs, her mother was in denial, her man was with another woman and her father had just been shot and killed. Although her whole world was crumbling down around her, she made a decision right then and there that she would stand and confront these issues that seemed to be attacking her. She would stand and fight for her sanity. She would not go under, she would survive. She would make it through this rough time in her life.

She looked over at Justine who was still pacing and praying. She got out of the bed and slowly started to walk. As she walked, she felt a new sense of strength. Then she started to pray. "Father God. I praise your name today. I thank you that although I am going through problems right now, I will survive. I pray that you will give me the strength to comfort my mother while she deals with the death of my father. I thank you for keeping me in my right mind through all of this. I pray that you will heal my sister. I pray that you will continue to use me to help women all over the world. I'm giving my counseling skills to you. Use them as you see fit. Now, Father. Please take care of Jennifer and her mother, and her husband. Help them to make it through this. This is my prayer. Amen."

She kept pacing as she thought about the fact that her father had lost his life over doing people wrong. What a price to pay. She kept thinking over and over again. What a price to pay.

The Funeral

Clara went to her mother's house on the day that she heard the news. She was a pillar of strength as she made the arrangements to bury her father. She called the local newspaper and had an obituary printed, then she called the funeral home and made an appointment to settle the details of the burial.

Loretta refused to have anything to do with it. She had even demanded that Clara leave her name out of the obituary and the programs for the funeral. On the day of the funeral, Clara was able to talk her into riding in the family car.

There were two cars, one with Clara, her mother and her sister and the other with Jennifer and her mother. Jennifer's husband was still in jail. They all sat on the front row and mourned the life and the death of her father.

Clara wanted to cry, but couldn't make any tears flow. She realized that she had stopped loving her father a long time ago. She had already mourned her loss during the first few years after he left them. The only thing to do now was to bury him and get it over with. She felt a twinge of guilt for feeling this way, but she immediately asked God to forgive her.

Her mother was crying hysterically while Loretta looked like she would rather be somewhere else. There were not many people at the funeral, just some of her father's relatives and a few of his buddies from work. Clara felt like they were all smirking at her because her father had been such a disgusting man. Even in death, Clara could find nothing much good about him. Her one good memory was of the time when her mother had to work a double shift and he had made them dinner - baked beans and bacon with some kind of maple syrup that tasted really good. Funny, the only good memory Clara had of her father was baked beans and bacon.

Jennifer and her mother just looked straight ahead. They both looked very sad and very lost. After the funeral, the family declined to have people over. Only the immediate family was invited to come to the house.

Clara, her mother and sister were sitting in the living room when the doorbell rang. When Clara opened the door, she was surprised to see Jennifer and her mother standing there.

"May we come in?" Jennifer's mother asked.

"Yes, please come in." Clara opened the door and stepped aside to let them in.

"Jennifer wanted to talk to you. She asked me to come with her."

Clara took a good look at Jennifer's mother. She was pale, very pale like she didn't get enough sun. Clara figured it was probably from all the years of being cooped up in her bedroom. The woman was very thin and nervous looking. She moved stiffly, as if each step was an effort. Clara wondered what it had been like for her holed up in that room all these years, knowing that her husband was sleeping with her daughter.

Clara carefully studied Jennifer, not sure if she should trust her.

"Clara, I'm sorry. I know I hurt you." Jennifer stood there awkwardly. "I was sick. I've been seeing a doctor and he's helping me to deal with this whole thing. I just wanted to say I'm sorry."

Clara nodded her head without saying a word.

"Clara, I think Jennie's gone," Jennifer whispered. "I haven't seen her since it happened."

Clara wondered if this could be true. She had heard of stuff like this happening all the time. Once the reason for the dual personality was gone, the mind began to make adjustments. Clara didn't know enough about Jennifer's illness to determine if Jennie could really be gone.

"Clara."

"What?" Clara realized that she was still upset with the girl.

"I'm really sorry," Jennifer apologized again. "And thank you, Clara. I mean it." She waited for Clara to say something. When Clara remained quiet, she looked at her mother. "Well, that's it. Come on Mom. Let's go."

"Thank you for all you've done for my daughter," the woman said before she turned and followed her daughter to the door. Once at the door, she turned around to face Clara and her family. "I hate to say it, but I'm glad he's gone. We went through hell in that house. Now we have to try to pull our lives together again."

Jennifer and her mother stood at the door. Jennifer opened the door and turned to Clara. "I hope that you and your family get through this okay. I'm sorry." She turned and walked out behind her mother, shutting the door behind them.

Clara looked at her sister and her mother. "I hope so too," she thought. "I really do hope that we can get through this." She watched her mother who was sitting on a chair in the living room, still crying. She had not stopped crying since she heard the news. Clara didn't know how to comfort her. She didn't know what to say. She walked over and put her arm around her mother's heaving shoulders.

"It's going to be okay, Mom." Was all she could bring herself to say.

Her sister stood looking at them. She seemed to be totally disgusted with her mother. She poured herself another drink. She was drinking more than usual, if that was possible.

Clara felt like screaming, but she stayed calm. She just wanted this to be over with. She just wanted to leave this house and never come back. She wanted to bury all of her memories and never dig them up again. But she knew that she had to deal with all of this and somehow make sense of it. Only then could she begin to heal and have a normal life.

"Momma! Why are you crying over that dead bastard?" Loretta screamed drunkenly. "Why are you even wasting your tears?"

Her mother stopped sobbing. Slowly she lifted her head and looked at Loretta. "I'm not crying for him." She wiped at her tears. "I'm crying for you."

Loretta and Clara both stopped what they were doing and stood there with their mouths open.

"I lost you because I didn't believe you when you told me what happened," their mother continued. "I'm so sorry." She started sobbing again. "Loretta, baby. I'm so sorry. I've wasted all of these years. I was never a real mother to you." Her voice broke as she spoke through her tears. "I accused you of messing up my life and you were the one who was suffering." Covering her face, she confessed, "I was only thinking about myself." Then she moved her hand and pleaded with her daughter. "Can you ever forgive me?"

Loretta stood there with her mouth still open for a minute before what her mother had said broke through her drunken haze. "Momma, are you saying that you believe me now?"

"Yes, baby," her mother wept, "I'm so sorry. I'm sorry for not believing you before. Please forgive me."

"Oh Momma. I do forgive you. Thank you, Momma, for believing me." Loretta ran crying into her mother's arms. Her mother held Loretta and rocked her back and forth like she was a baby.

Clara cried as she watched her mother and her sister. This was the first time she had seen her mother hug her sister since they were children. It was good to see them hugging each other and weeping with the sorrow of lost yesterdays and the joy that tomorrow was promising to bring. Today they had buried her father, but they had also had a funeral for the bitterness and resentment that had been a part of her family for so long. Clara sighed with relief. Her family was beginning a new journey. Clara knew that they had a long way to go, but she was prepared to be there every step of the way. Clara left them there holding each other while she went into the other room to call Francine. She had buried her mother today, and Clara wanted to give her condolences. She felt overjoyed that a day of great loss was tinged with hope.

New Beginnings

A few days later, Clara sat in her office. She smiled at the pretty woman sitting across from her. Lauren looked absolutely gorgeous. Clara couldn't believe that this was the same woman who had come into her office so upset a couple of weeks ago.

Lauren had on a very pretty dress, and her hair and makeup were done just right. She had lost a few pounds, which only added to her beauty.

Clara noticed that there was a glow about her, almost as if she was in love. Clara hoped that she had not gotten back with Tony.

"Clara, you won't believe what has happened since I last saw you." Lauren couldn't hide her excitement. "I went to a party at my cousin's house and ran into someone who I had not seen in years."

Clara sat quietly, enjoying Lauren's happiness.

"I was still kind of depressed about what happened with Tony and was just sitting on the couch trying not to be noticed. Then I heard a familiar voice and when I looked up, I couldn't believe my eyes."

Clara smiled as Lauren recalled the events of the night of the party.

"I looked up into the face of the most handsome guy I've seen in a long time," Lauren continued. "The funny thing was I couldn't place the face. I knew the voice, but the face was different. He had the most beautiful eyes." She fanned herself with her right hand. "Then he asked me if I remembered him and right at that moment, I remembered who he was." She paused as if to collect her thoughts. "We were friends in grade school and he used to have such a crush on me. He would wait for me after class and carry my books for me." Lauren's laughter filled the room. "He was always late for his classes and he would take off running down the hall to try to make it before the bell."

Clara laughed with Lauren.

"It was the cutest thing," Lauren said with an amused look on her face.

"Well, it looks like you've had a blast from the past." Clara couldn't help laughing. "So, what's going on with this guy?"

"Well....we've been seeing each other for the last couple of weeks, and it's the strangest thing but I think I'm falling for him." Lauren's eyes lit up as she shared this with Clara. "I never liked him like that in school. He was just a nerd that carried my books."

"Nerd? He doesn't sound like a nerd to me."

"That's just it. He's changed. Gone are the big thick glasses and the bucked teeth. Gone are the plaid shirts and the high water pants. Gone is the skinny little kid who the wind could blow away."

"Replaced by?"

"He had corrective surgery to fix his vision and he also fixed his teeth. He must have been reading GQ because he looks like he could be a model for them. Actually, he's quite a hunk now." Lauren held her hand over her heart and smiled a great big smile. "A very good looking hunk if I may say so."

"How does he feel about you?"

"That's just it. He says that he has never stopped thinking about me. He said that he only came to the party hoping that I would be there."

"Where has he been all of these years?"

"It seems that he built a very successful company and got married. The marriage lasted about five years and he says that he was so hurt by his ex-wife that he buried himself in his work after they split up." Then one day a few weeks ago, he heard that my cousin was giving a party and he came looking for me."

"Last question." Clara had to ask one more question before Lauren went any further. "How does your daughter get along with him?"

Lauren's face beamed brighter. "She absolutely adores him. And he's so good with her. He says he loves her because she is a part of me and he knows that she must be special because I am."

As Clara sat listening, her heart started to beat faster. It seemed like Lauren had found true love and although Clara was happy for her, she felt sad. Her heart ached for this type of love. Her heart ached for the love that she had lost. If only she had not messed things up with Jason. She shook her head to stop herself from going down this road again. She wished that she could just forget about Jason. Jason was gone. She might as well face it. Gone.

"Clara, aren't you happy for me?"

"Oh yes. I'm very happy that you have found the love of your life. I'm especially happy that he gets along with your daughter and that your daughter likes him."

"Well then, what's wrong?"

Clara started to say that everything was fine. Then she decided to tell Lauren. "I was thinking that I once had a love like that, a very special love. Only, I had too many personal problems to recognize it for what it was and I lost it."

"Oh, I'm sorry. And here I am bragging about how great my guy is."

"Listen, don't you feel bad." Clara waved her hand. "You should be happy that you've finally found someone who cares about you in the way that you deserve to be cared about." She smiled at Lauren as she went on. "This guy sounds like a real nice guy." Clara looked Lauren in the eyes. "Promise me that you'll never, ever settle for less."

"I promise. Can you believe that Tony has been sending me candy and flowers at my office?" She rolled her eyes at the ceiling. "He sends me emails and says that he wants me back in his life."

Clara was not surprised by Tony's behavior. This was typical for men like him. She only hoped that

Lauren would just stay away from him. "Are you still seeing him?" Clara had to ask.

"I only saw him once to tell him that I would have him arrested if he ever came near me or called me again. I mean it. I will not tolerate any man who mistreats my daughter in any way." The giggles were gone. She had a serious expression on her face as she spoke. "I'm going forward with my life. It's time for a new beginning."

Clara nodded. "That sounds like a good idea to me. A new beginning."

"Well, I have to go." Lauren stood up. "I'm meeting my guy for lunch."

"Okay." Clara stood and walked Lauren to the door. When they got to the door, she gave the girl a hug. "You take care of yourself. I'm really happy for you."

"Thanks." Lauren returned Clara's hug, patting her on the back. "Don't worry. If your guy was really meant to be, he'll be back."

"Thanks." Clara sure hoped so.

"Okay. Bye." Lauren floated out the door.

Clara stood there for a moment wondering if what Lauren had just said could be true. She shook her head at the thought of little Lauren giving her advice about love. That girl had grown a lot as a result of her experiences with Tony. Clara walked over to her desk and stared at the picture of her and Jason that she still kept on her desk. Lauren could be right. Only time would tell.

Patricia And Brian

Later that afternoon, Clara was sitting in her office when the phone rang. "Hello. Clara speaking."

"Hello, Clara."

Clara almost fainted when she heard Jason's voice.

"Clara. Are you still there?"

"Yes. I'm sorry. I...I'm here."

"I heard about your father. I'm sorry."

Clara wondered how he had heard. She had purposely not told any of their mutual friends. She didn't want him to feel obligated to come to the funeral. Besides she would have had a hard time facing him anyway. "Thanks, Jason, Thanks for calling."

"I'm here for you. If you need anything, just call me."

Tears rolled down her cheeks.

"Clara."

"I'm here." Clara tried to keep her voice steady.

"I mean it," Jason told her. "If you need me. Call me."

"I will." Clara wanted to tell him right then that she did need him. But she couldn't. She wasn't ready. She had to take things one step at a time.

"Clara, I hate us being like this. I wish we could work things out."

"Jason, I'm sorry. My next client is waiting. I have to go. Thanks again for calling, Jason." Clara hung up the phone and shook her head in disbelief. Jason still cared. He sounded really good. Her first instinct had been to hang up the phone, but when she realized that he was just paying his respects, she let him talk. Clara was fine until he started talking about working things out. What was he thinking about? What was he going to do with pretty little Monica? Clara couldn't think about that. It was over between her and Jason. Wasn't it? Clara thought again about what Lauren had said about love that was meant to be.

Just then the phone buzzed and it was Sandra telling her that her next appointment was ready.

"Show her in," she said as she got up to meet Patricia at the door. She was surprised to see that Patricia had someone with her.

"Hi Patricia. Come on in." She backed up to let them by.

"Clara, this is my husband Brian." Patricia was smiling as she introduced the man who was guilty of beating her up for the past three years.

"Oh. Hello." Clara tried to contain the anger that was boiling up in her chest. "Brian, Patricia, have a seat." She gestured towards the couch.

Brian and Patricia sat down on the couch next to each other holding hands. Clara noticed that Patricia seemed happier than usual and she didn't have a black eye or a busted lip today. Clara sensed that something had changed.

"Clara, I wanted to bring Brian to my appointment today. Yesterday I went with him to his anger management class and they suggested that he come with me today."

"Okay," Clara thought, "so he's taking anger management classes."

"Clara, I know that you don't think that Patricia should be with me." Brian spoke for the first time. "But I really love her and I realize that I've been wrong for beating her up all these years."

Clara squinted her eyes at Brian trying to determine if he was for real.

"I want her to continue seeing you. I would also like you to know that I'm seeing a counselor in addition to AA and anger management classes."

"That's a lot of things going on." Clara tried not to show him that she was impressed.

"I will do everything I can to keep my wife."

"Well," Clara thought, "he sounds sincere. But then they always do."

"I really do love her and I'm going to learn how to treat her right." Brian actually had tears in his eyes as he spoke. "I almost lost her. She just packed up one day and left me. I couldn't live with that." He shifted on the couch and was now holding both of Patricia's hands. "She's so precious to me. More than my own life."

213

Clara wondered if the couple on the couch could be for real. They were now looking into each other's eyes, smiling. Again, she felt the pitter, patter of her heart. She felt twinges of the pain of losing Jason. She had to get a grip.

"Well, I certainly am happy that you've seen the light, Brian. No woman deserves to be beaten."

"You're right. No woman deserves to go through what my wife went through with me. I was having a hard time at work and I couldn't seem to pay the bills. Then I was drinking too much and I just blew it." He stopped and looked at his wife. "But this woman has seen it in her heart to give me another chance, and I'm going to do everything that I can to make sure that I don't blow it this time."

Clara sat back and thought about what he had just said. She wondered what had happened to change him from a wife beating drunk to a man that wanted to get his life together. Situations like this rarely turned around. "Patricia, how do you feel about all of this?"

Patricia's smile told the story. "Brian knows that I won't allow him to beat me anymore. You've helped me to see that I'm much too valuable for that, but I know that this situation is out of my hands. Only God can help Brian to change his life."

"Yeah," Brian jumped in. "I'm taking anger management classes over at the church and Patricia and I have started going to service together on Sunday." He paused as he thought about his next words. "Somehow, my outlook on life has been changed. I don't really know how to explain it, but

I'm not so worried about things anymore. Like Patricia says, it's out of our hands. God is in control now."

That's it! Clara thought. Men like this rarely changed, but Brian had turned to God for help. That explained it. "Well, Brian. I must tell you that I never thought I'd say this, but I hope everything works out for you and Patricia."

Brian nodded. "Thanks, Clara. That means a lot coming from you. You know what we've been through. So it means a lot to have you pulling for us."

"Well I am pulling for you," Clara assured him. "And I believe that you can do just what you say you want to do."

"Thank you."

"Thanks, Clara." Patricia kept smiling.

Clara sat there watching the two of them. They were glowing like they had just fallen in love.

Lauren had found a new love and Patricia had renewed her love with her husband. Clara wondered what would happen next.

Monica's Heart

As Clara walked Patricia and Brian out to the reception area, she thought about her day. Lauren was doing fine with the guy who had a crush on her in grade school and Patricia and Brian were going to church together and trying to make their marriage work. She remembered how she used to think that she was not helping anyone. It seemed to her that once she dealt with her own issues, the door was opened for her to help these women who had been coming to her for years. Since she had faced her past, she felt free for the first time in her life. She didn't have to worry that someone would find out about her childhood and judge her because of what had happened. It was all in the open now and even her mother had started to act differently towards her and Loretta.

Clara no longer felt like she couldn't do anything right, and her mother and sister were spending a lot of time together. She stood in the doorway of her office and watched Patricia and Brian exit through the glass doors of the Center. Brian walked Patricia over to the passenger side of the car and opened the door for her. Once she was safely inside, he closed the door and hurried around to the driver's side and got in.

Still gazing out into the parking lot, Clara chuckled to herself as she thought about the way her mother fussed over Loretta. Her mother treated Loretta like a little girl, buying her clothes and taking her out to lunch and the movies. Clara could tell that Loretta loved the attention. She was beginning to take better care of herself and Clara believed that she had cut down on drinking and using drugs.

As Clara stood there thinking about her sister and her mother, a car pulled into the parking lot of the Center. Clara wanted to run and hide when she saw Monica get out of the car and walk towards the Center. She stepped back into her office and closed the door. She walked quickly to her desk and sat down. Her heart was pounding. What was Monica doing here? Maybe she had come to see one of the counselors. Why would she come here to see her? Clara wondered how Monica knew where she worked.

Clara sat there and hoped that her worst nightmare wasn't coming true. She certainly didn't want to see Monica, not on official or unofficial business. Clara jumped when her phone rang. She looked at the phone as if it could bite her. "Come on, Clara," she told herself. "You're not afraid. Answer the phone." She picked up the phone.

"Yes, Sandra?"

"Clara, there's a lady out here who's insisting that you see her."

"Who is it?" Clara wanted to be sure.

"She says that her name is Monica. Just Monica."

"Okay. I'm coming to get her." Clara hung up the phone and stood up. Taking a deep breath, she wondered again what Monica could possibly want with her.

"Okay. Here goes nothing." She walked slowly to the door. She stopped for a moment, and then she opened the door and stood face to face with Monica. "Come in," Clara said as she stood back from the door.

Monica walked in and Clara closed the door.

"Have a seat." Clara waved towards the seating area as she walked over and sat behind her desk. She felt that was the safest place for her to be.

"Okay. We don't have to play games. What are you doing here?"

"I'm here because of Jason." Monica continued to stand, pacing back in forth in front of Clara's desk.

Jason. Clara didn't like the sound of Jason's name coming out of Monica's mouth.

"I want you to know that I care a lot about Jason," Monica said as she sat down and crossed her legs.

Clara felt like she was playing a part in a bad movie in which the woman who has the man confronts the woman the man used to date. "Okay. I'll ask you again. Why are you here?" Clara couldn't believe how pretty Monica was. She had only seen her once, and she remembered thinking then that she was pretty, but this woman was really beautiful. Everything about her was perfect. Her hair, her teeth, her skin, her nails, even the way she dressed.

"Clara, you don't understand. I really care about Jason. As a matter of fact, I'm in love with him."

There went Clara's heart again. Thumping like it was going to burst through her chest. Clara felt like she was going to have a heart attack. Why was Monica torturing her like this? She didn't need to hear the details of her love affair with Jason. Besides she and Jason were over. Didn't this woman know that? Or was she too pretty to be smart too?

"Listen, Clara. I want Jason. Actually, he's everything that I need in a man. He's kind and loving and generous..."

"Stop it!" Clara couldn't take any more. "You can have Jason. Jason and I broke up some time ago. I thought you knew that." She felt her heart crumbling into little pieces. "I don't know why you felt it was necessary for you to come in here to tell me about your undying love for a man who is not even a part of my life anymore." Clara fought to hold back the tears. "You can have him. Is that what you came to hear?" Clara glared at Monica. "Now, if you don't mind, I need you to leave." Clara was trying hard to keep her composure. She certainly didn't want Monica to see her cry.

"I do mind." Monica leaned forward and picked up the picture of Jason and Clara from the desk. She looked at it closely and put it down again. "And I'm not leaving until you hear what I have to say."

Clara couldn't believe the nerve of this girl.

"Clara, as I told you, I love Jason. I would love to marry him." She stopped and looked at Clara as though to see if she was listening. "I have been

219

waiting to see what you were going to do about your relationship with him, but I'm tired of waiting. I wanted to let you know that I'm getting ready to go after him with everything that I have in me."

Clara's heart was still going crazy.

"We've talked about you and the man is still in love with you. I came here to give you one last chance to come to your senses. If you don't talk to him and resolve matters between the two of you, I'm going after him." She stood up and placed both hands on Clara's desk. She leaned over and put her face right in front of Clara's. Locking eyes with her she continued, "And let me tell you one more thing. Once I set my mind on something, I usually get what I want."

"Why are you doing this then?" Clara didn't like Monica in her face. She pushed her chair back to put some distance between them. "Why even bother to come here? Why don't you just go ahead and get Jason? You already told me that you love him and that you want him."

Monica was still leaning over Clara's desk. "I didn't come here for you, silly lady. I came here because I want Jason to be happy." She straightened up and turned to pick her purse up from the couch. "I could have him if I want him, but he is so in love with you, that I would have to spend too much time trying to get his mind off of you." Monica stood up straight and smoothed her skirt around her hips with her hands. "Besides, as selfish as I am, I've never wanted someone else's man. But if you don't want him, that's a different story." She started towards the door.

Clara wanted to scream for her to wait, to ask her if she had really meant what she said about Jason still being in love with her. She opened her mouth to talk but no sound came out. Clara tried to get up and run after Monica, but she couldn't move. She could only watch as Monica opened the door and left her office, never even looking back.

Second Chances

As Clara sat frozen at her desk she thought about what had just happened. Suddenly she was angry, then puzzled, and finally afraid of what would happen next. She stood up on wobbly legs and walked over to the window. She looked out of the window at nothing in particular. Suddenly, she felt the need to get out of there. She turned and grabbed her purse and ran out the door.

As she ran, Sandra called out that she had an appointment with someone named Lisa that afternoon. Clara stopped in her tracks and turned to look at Sandra.

"Sandra, Lisa is a sweet little girl that I met at the movies the other night. I asked her to come in here today," Clara explained as she tried to figure out what to do.

Sandra just sat there looking at Clara with a silly expression on her face.

Clara laughed, "I know. I know. You want to know what I'm doing running out the door if I have an appointment with this girl."

Sandra half nodded her head.

"Sandra, I really need to get out of here. I can't stay here any longer today." Clara paused to think for a minute. Listen, I want you to sit down and interview Lisa when she gets here. Give her a real interview. You know. Make it appear real, at least. And then give her a job."

Sandra smiled at Clara.

"A part-time job," Clara remembered to add. "I'll have to pay her. At least at first, but that's okay. She needs something to do to keep her busy." Clara paused again as she remembered Sandra's daughter. She regretted that she had not thought to give her a part-time job after school.

"It's okay," Sandra interrupted her thoughts. "My little girl is going to be fine. She's having the baby. She still wants to get married but she's too young for that. I told her that if they still want to get married in a few years I'll sign for her."

Clara nodded and took a step towards Sandra.

"No, don't come over here hugging on me trying to get me all worked up again." Sandra was back to normal. "I'll be fine, and I'll give little Ms. Lisa enough to do to keep her out of trouble." Sandra organized the papers on her desk. "I could use some help around here anyway. As a matter of fact, she can start today."

"Yeah, that's a good idea. Tell her to come in everyday after school. Tell her that I'll see her tomorrow." Clara put her hand on the door and then stopped and turned around again. "Oh, and Sandra?"

"Yes?" Sandra asked.

"Thanks," Clara told her. "Thanks for all of your help. I don't know what I'd do without you."

Sandra just stood there, not saying a word as a tear escaped and streamed down her face.

Clara smiled at her and waved. Then she turned and pulled open the door. As soon as she stepped outside, she felt free. Free to do whatever she wanted to do. Free from the walls of the clinic that sometimes seemed to yell out at her. Free from the paperwork that still had to be completed for the clients that she had seen today. She didn't want to think about any of that right now. She just wanted to be out here with nature, closer to God. She got into her car and started the engine. For a moment, as she thought about going home, she felt a sense of panic. She didn't want to go home. There was nothing there. Just an empty house with walls that seemed to scream out to her, telling her to do things that she no longer wanted to do. She seemed to be fighting a battle with the walls wherever she went. Walls that were trying to box her in and hold her captive to the things that she was still breaking free from. Walls that wanted her to keep drinking, and walls that wanted her to keep feeling sorry for her self. Walls that wanted her to hate, and walls that wanted her to be afraid. No, Clara couldn't go home. She needed some time to think.

Clara turned the corner and headed for the park that was close to her house. She parked under her favorite tree and reached for the bag that she had gotten from the store earlier that day. She pulled out the bottle of coke and screwed open the top. She opened the glove compartment and pulled out a straw. Clara sat and sipped the lukewarm soda and watched the children play. She remembered how much fun she and Loretta used to have in this very same park. They would laugh and play with their friends until the sun was low in the sky. Then they would run home and race up the steps to their house hoping that their mother and father would still be busy with their friends.

As Clara thought about her childhood years, she noticed that the usual feelings of anxiety and despair were gone. She felt free to wander through the difficult times of her childhood and not become upset or afraid. Clara settled back in the leather seat of her car and let out a sigh of relief. She smiled as she realized that she was finally free. The buried secrets that had kept her from enjoying life to the fullest had been revealed. Her mind was no longer playing games on her. She was no longer angry, bitter, or afraid. She felt like a new woman. She really felt like her life had changed.

Clara remembered the night that Jason had left the house. She was in this very same park getting drunk before going home to fight with him. The memories were so painful that day that she'd kept drinking in order to block them out. She was drunk when she went home and that was the night that Jason met Monica. Monica had walked into her office today to tell her that she loved Jason and that she wanted him for herself. Clara felt herself getting angry. Monica had a lot of nerve coming into her office like that. Clara remembered what Monica had said. She had said that she didn't want someone else's man. She had insinuated that Jason was still in love with her. Clara picked up her cell phone from its holder and dialed Jason's number.

"Hello." Monica's voice came over the phone line.

"Hello, Monica. It's Clara. Is Jason there?"

Monica sighed loudly into the receiver. "Somehow I was hoping that you would be foolish enough *not* to call. Hold on."

"Hello." Jason's voice spoke into Clara's ear.

Clara's heart beat louder and faster, keeping a steady rhythm.

"Hello." Jason spoke a little louder.

"Jason. It's Clara." Clara felt stupid as she wondered why she had bothered to call.

"Clara. I'm glad to hear from you. Are you okay?" Jason was always so thoughtful. Always making sure that she was okay. Clara remembered how she used to hate it when he asked her that. As if he could do anything if she wasn't okay. But today, she was glad to hear him ask this familiar question. Glad that he still cared.

"Yes, everything's okay. As a matter of fact, things are getting better everyday." She tried to hide her nervousness.

"Good. I'm glad to hear that."

"Listen, Jason. I'm sorry to call your house and disrespect your girlfriend. I would never do that. Except I needed to talk to you."

"Monica is not my girlfriend. She's my buddy's sister. When you kicked me out, I came to stay with him and she lives right next door." His tone was teasing. "Although I think she has a crush on me. She's always hanging around. Cooking and cleaning for us." Jason chuckled. "Her brother's such a slob. He makes you look neat."

"Are you suggesting that I'm sloppy?" Clara teased back.

"No. I wasn't saying that." Jason's tone was defensive.

Clara smiled into the phone. She realized that she had been much too serious in their relationship. Jason didn't even know when she was joking. As a matter of fact, it had been a long time since she had joked with him.

"Ease up." She laughed out loud. "I was just joking."

Jason laughed too.

Clara held the phone and thought about how good it was to make him laugh again.

"Clara."

"Jason."

They both spoke at once. Clara felt warm all over as feelings of love for Jason swept over her entire being. She had always loved Jason, but she had never felt this way before. At that moment, she knew that Jason was the man for her.

"Clara."

She let Jason speak.

"I need to see you."

"I was just thinking the same thing myself."

"Where are you?"

"I'm in the park around the corner from my house. Can you meet me at my house?"

"I'm on my way."

"I'll be waiting."

"Until then."

"Until then." Clara pressed the button to end the call.

She sat back and hugged herself tight. "I love you," she told herself for the first time in her life. She laughed as she said it again, "I love you, Clara. I love you."

She was almost hilarious with the feelings of joy that were sweeping over her. She sat there and savored the moment. Then she started the car. Jason was going to be at her house in a few minutes. Clara wanted to sit down and have a long talk with him about all that had happened since he left. Most importantly, she was going to tell him how much she missed him and how much she loved him. She turned on the radio and began singing along with the music. As she turned the corner, she saw Jason's car pull into her driveway. When she pulled in behind him, he was getting out of the car. As she put her car in park, he was already heading towards her.

She jumped out of her car and ran into his arms.

He grabbed her and held her tight.

"Oh Jason, I have so much to tell you." She felt like she was dreaming. He looked so good. Clara was in heaven as he held her tight. The scent of his cologne was driving her crazy.

"There's only one thing that I want you to tell me." He looked into her eyes as he spoke.

"What's that?"

"Tell me that you'll marry me. That you'll be my wife."

Clara's heart was beating faster, then even faster. She wondered if Jason could feel it as he held her. Her palms were sweating and her mouth got really dry.

"Jason."

Jason released her just a little.

"Jason, I want to tell you so much. I want to tell you that I missed you."

Jason was shaking his head from side to side.

Clara knew that he wanted her to stop but she still had so much to say. "Jason, I was really messed up, and I want to tell you that I'm sorry for saying that my business was nobody's business." Clara kept talking. "I want to tell you everything. I want to share everything with you."

"What did you say?"

"I said I want to share everything with you. My heart, my soul and my life." Clara thought she heard music, like the sound of angels singing.

"Clara."

"Shhhhhh." She put her finger on his lips. "You talk too much." She smiled up at him. "Tonight I'm going to talk for a change." She kissed him lightly on the lips. "Yes, Jason. I will marry you. I want to be your wife. I want to spend the rest of my life with you."

"Yahoo!" Jason laughed as he swept her off her feet and swung her around in the driveway. "Yes! She's going to be my wife!"

"Jason. You're making me dizzy," Clara laughed. She had never been this happy before.

Jason put her down and leaned down to kiss her on the lips.

Clara might have been imagining things, but she could hear cheering and clapping. "That must be the angels again, rejoicing because we're back together." She thought to herself as she swooned in her future husband's arms. While they kissed, the neighbors kept on clapping and cheering.

A few minutes later, Jason and Clara made their way into the house. They sat at the kitchen table and talked for hours. Jason pulled his chair to the same side of the table as Clara's. He sat facing her, holding her hands and looking into her eyes as she told him about all that had happened since he left.

When she got to the part about her father, she started crying. She wanted to stop and keep this part to herself, but she knew that the only way for her to have total truth in her marriage with Jason was by being honest and open with him.

Jason listened intently to what Clara was saying.

Clara wondered what he was thinking as she told him about the gory details of her childhood and how guilty she had felt for keeping this family secret for so long. She looked down at her lap as she spoke, afraid of what she might see if she looked into Jason's eyes. But she continued. Telling him about her fears and how she had never felt like she was good enough for him. She told him about her sister and how she now understood why they never got along. She told him about her mother and how she was unaware of the anger that she had harbored against the woman who had brought her into the world. She told him about Jeff and how she ran into him at the Video store. She even told him about the night she spent on the couch with Jeff, watching movies.

She felt Jason tense up as she told him about Jeff. She had met Jason six months after Jeff left for Atlanta. She had still not been over her breakup with him at the time, and she remembered telling Jason all about Jeff and her love for him.

"You mean to tell me that you spent the night with Jeff and nothing happened?" Jason squinted his eyes and Clara got ready to be interrogated.

"Yes," she nodded. "I was so broken up over losing you and I just needed someone to talk to." She wondered if he believed her.

"I believe you. Now do you believe that nothing happened with me and Monica?"

Clara nodded her head. "Yes. I believe you."

"And that nothing happened with Faye either?"

Clara's head shot up to look at Jason. "Faye?"

"Yeah. You know about Faye," Jason reminded her. "She's the woman I met the night I left after our fight."

Clara was shaking her head. "No, that was Monica."

Jason chuckled. "Oh, you thought that Monica was the woman I told you about." He reached for Clara's hands.

Without thinking, Clara pulled away.

"Oh, come on, honey. Don't tell me that you're going to freak out over some woman that I spent some time with."

"Some time? Some time? What do you mean, some time?" She fought to control the tone of her voice.

"Yes. Some time. What did you want me to do? You kicked me out of your life, and it didn't look like you were going to take me back."

"I don't believe this! Here I am, thinking that we can get back together and you've been spending time with not one woman, but two."

"Oh, my god," Jason said, holding his head in his hands. "You have not changed one bit." He glared at her. "You sure had me fooled for a minute." He stood up and began to pace around the table. "You brought me over here and told me that you'd marry me." He walked faster and faster around the table. "Now, you want to freak out on me because I made a friend."

"A friend? Okay, if she's just a friend, then she won't mind if you don't see her anymore."

"What are you saying? Now you want me to just tell this woman that I can't be her friend anymore?"

"Yes. Jason, if you love me and we're going to be married, I need you to cut all ties with both this Faye woman and Monica."

"Monica's a baby. And Faye is a very nice lady who took time with me when you wouldn't."

Clara didn't like the way that sounded. She wondered just how close Jason was to this woman.

"Jason, just how close are you to this woman? How much time did you two spend together?"

Jason stopped pacing. He stood in front of Clara and looked down at his hand, which was making imaginary circles on the table. "Listen Clara, I think I'd better leave."

"Leave? No, I don't think you should leave. You always leave when the going gets tough. If we're going to be married, you have to learn how to stay and fight." Clara took a deep breath. "Now tell me. How much time did you spend with this woman?"

"This is not necessary." Jason tried to walk away, but Clara grabbed his wrist. "Clara, it's in the past." He looked down at her hand holding his. "Okay, if you want them out, they're out."

Clara shook her head as she let go of his wrist. "No, Jason. I don't think that's the answer. She stood up and touched his chin as she looked up at him. "I told you that the only way we're going to make it is if we're honest." She tried to smile. "Now, I think there's something you're not telling me."

Jason opened his mouth to say something.

"No. Don't say anything." Clara stopped him. "I have told you everything. You know that nothing happened with me and Jeff." She waved her hand in a wide sweeping gesture. "As a matter of fact, he's out of my life." Clara sat down and crossed her legs, thinking about her last words. Then she went on, "Monica came into my office and told me that she was in love with you."

Jason looked surprised.

"I called you because I knew you had not been intimate with her and I felt we still had a chance. Now we have someone else involved, and you seem to be reluctant to tell me about your relationship with her." Clara fought back the tears. "There is one thing I learned from this whole experience."

Jason moved from one foot to the other.

Clara didn't like the way he was acting. She had to stop herself from getting angry. After all, she was the one who had thrown him out. She was the one who had been too messed up to notice what she had in him. But she couldn't bear the thought of him with another woman. More than that, she couldn't bear to have him lie to her. Honesty was the most important thing to her right now.

"I learned that I am somebody special. I have started to heal in certain areas of my life." She noticed that Jason was staring at her with a strange look on his face. "Do you understand what I'm saying to you?"

Jason nodded. "I think so."

"I want to make it perfectly clear. I must have total honesty in a relationship. I cannot deal with lies or deception." She stared intently back at him. At this moment, she wished that she could read his mind.

"Clara, I...I need time to think."

Clara's heart sank, but she steadied herself. She fought to maintain her composure. "What do you mean time?" She was fighting to keep her voice steady.

"All of this came so suddenly. For the past few weeks, you wanted absolutely nothing to do with me." He paused and looked around the kitchen. "Now, out of the blue, you call me and you want to get married." He let out a deep breath. "I need some time to get my thoughts together."

It was Clara's turn to sigh now. She took a deep breath and prayed for the strength to make it through this. She looked at Jason and noticed that he was watching her closely again.

"Are you okay?"

"Yes, I am. You see, Jason. I don't have to convince you that I've changed. But something strange has happened to me, something wonderful." She smiled shakily. "I do love you, and I want to marry you someday. But not until you're ready to be in an honest, open, committed relationship with someone like me."

"Clara, you know that I love you."

"That is only the beginning of what it will take to be married to me. Why don't you go home now?"

"Are you kicking me out again?"

"Absolutely not. I just need you to be sure." She smiled at him, feeling joy in her heart. "I don't want to be with a man just to say I'm married. I can't settle for less anymore."

Jason was looking at her as if he was seeing her for the first time.

"Why are you looking at me like that? Are you okay?"

He half nodded, half shook his head.

Clara, not sure of whether he meant yes or no reached out to touch his cheek. "I think I understand what you mean. Listen, I'm really tired. I need to get some rest." She walked over to the door and opened it as he walked towards her. "Give me a call."

He stopped and leaned over to kiss her. As they kissed, her soul cried out for him. She wanted to ask him not to go. But she knew that he had to leave.

"Bye, Clara." He walked past her, leaving her standing there with her heart beating twice its normal speed.

"Bye." She closed the door. She stood there crying silent tears as she thought about the past few hours. She tried to figure out where the night had gone wrong. One moment they were in the driveway, kissing and laughing. The next, they were at the kitchen table having this serious conversation about some woman that Clara had never even heard about.

That was just it. How could Jason not tell her about this woman? She could not stand to have any more secrets in her life. If Jason wanted to be with her, he had to come clean. She needed to know that no deep dark secret would come to haunt them years down the road. She was tired of secrets. If Jason had something with this woman, she had to know about it. She just wouldn't deal with secrets anymore. Clara walked into the living room and sat down.

"Boy. What a day," she thought as she picked up the remote and turned on the television set. Then she sat back and reflected on how her life had changed. She was sure she would never be the same again. In spite of all that had happened that day, she knew that she would make it with or without Jason.

The Seminar

A week later, Clara stood in front of the room full of women wondering what she was doing there.

Shortly after Jason left, Justine called her to ask her if she would speak at the seminar that she and her partner were giving the following week. Her partner was called out of town and wouldn't be back for a couple of weeks, and Justine needed Clara to speak to the group of women that were signed up for the seminar. It was a free seminar and Justine told Clara to invite anyone she wanted.

Clara agreed to speak at the seminar. Then she picked up the phone and invited her mother and her sister. She even called Sandra and invited her to bring her daughter and Lisa. They all agreed to come, and Clara felt a sense of excitement at having been chosen to speak. In all of her years of counseling, she had never spoken to a large group before.

She was surprised when she arrived to see that the seminar was being held in the largest conference room of the hotel. Justine told her that the room held five hundred people and they were booked solid. Clara tried not to be nervous as she stood and looked out at all the women that were filling up the room. A few days ago, Justine had faxed her a list of topics to choose from. Clara had looked at the list and thought about calling Justine to tell her she couldn't do it. Just as she was about to call, one of the topics jumped out at her. *Issues That Haunt Us.* Her heart beat faster as she decided that this would be her topic.

Now as she stood waiting to speak, she looked out at the beautiful faces of the women that were already seated. God had created each one with a unique beauty that was all her own. Clara's eyes filled up with tears as she thought about the issues that these women were faced with everyday.

Just then, she heard Justine introducing her. She walked over to the podium and began to speak.

"Good evening. My name is Clara Walton. I have been asked to speak to you today about the issues that haunt us." She paused and looked around the room. "There are so many issues that we all face. We have to deal with our childhood issues. Some of us were neglected. Some of us were physically or sexually abused. Some of us were emotionally abused or abandoned by someone we love. Most of the issues that we dealt with in childhood are the ones that have determined who we are as adults. I had a troubled childhood. My sister and I went through a lot for little girls. My parents were alcoholics. My father fought my mother all of the time, and then one day, he left us."

Clara heard herself speaking, but she could not believe that she was actually telling her business to these strange women.

"As a result of my messed up childhood, I grew up to be messed up as an adult. I had all kinds of relationship problems. I couldn't keep a man." Clara laughed. "As a matter of fact, I still don't have a man."

The audience laughed with her.

"But, that's okay," She continued. "Because, you see, I have found out what the problem was. And one day, I stopped running from my past and embraced my future."

The women applauded.

"I was very sick. Inside." Clara patted her belly with her right hand. "I was needy, looking for a man to complete me. In the process of depending on the men in my life to make me happy, I was miserable." Clara smiled. "You see, what I had to do was find out why I was so needy. I had to find out why I couldn't trust myself to be happy in a relationship." She chuckled. "No relationship could stand up under the sabotage I brought against it. I did everything I could to run each and every man who tried to get close to me away."

She looked around the room and smiled when she saw her mother and her sister sitting in the fifth row smiling at her. Not far from them she spotted Sandra and her daughter sitting with Lisa.

"One day, I realized that I needed help," she continued. "Here I am a counselor and there are some of my clients here today." She said as she recognized Lauren and Patricia sitting in the audience. "I was trying to help other people, but I was getting nowhere because I had this great big issue in my own life." Clara paused and looked at several women in the audience. "I was trying to handle my issues on my own. Just like you." She pointed at one of the women in the audience. "And you." She looked out and connected with various women. "And definitely you."

A hush fell over the crowd, each woman afraid that her issue would be uncovered.

"I realized that I needed help, and I got it," Clara went on. "I found a friend, and she helped me to learn to lean on God. My life has not been the same since." Clara's eyes filled with tears. "I'm crying right now. But, I'm not crying because I'm sad. I'm crying because I'm happy. I'm crying because I'm free of the issues that have haunted me."

The women applauded again.

"Now, each one of you has to make a decision to look at your issue head on and say to that thing, you're not going to haunt me anymore." Clara's voice rose as she instructed the women to command their issues to leave them alone. "You must say, incest or whatever the name of your issue is, I'm not going to run from you anymore. I'm going to face you right now. So, come on." She backed up and put up her fists.

The women were on their feet.

"Tell that issue that you're taking back your life and tell that issue that it has no more power over you." Clara lowered her voice. "Once you do that, you'll be on your way to being free, and one thing that I must tell you is that you don't have to do this on your own. God is there to help you. And He'll be there to help you when you feel yourself begin to slip back into your old ways. All you have to do is ask Him and He'll be there for you." Clara looked around at the women again before going on. "You don't have to do it by yourself and you're never alone."

Clara straightened her notes on the podium. "Finally, I want to tell each and every one of you that you are special. You are all wonderfully and fearfully made, and each and every one of you is beautiful to behold." Clara smiled. "I know, because I'm looking at you."

The audience laughed as Clara continued. "Just remember that it doesn't matter what happened in your past. Starting today, you can move beyond your past to a wonderful future." She picked up her notes and stood clutching them to her chest. "Don't let anyone tell you that you deserve to be treated badly or beaten or cheated on or that it's your fault that some adult violated you as a child. That's a lie. Whatever you've been through or whatever you're going through today, you can make it. Especially with God on your side, you can make it. Whatever you do, just remember to keep your head up and walk tall and proud like the queens that you are. God bless you and thank you."

The women applauded as Clara walked back to her seat on wobbly legs. She felt weak. How could she stand up there and say what she said to these women. Yet, somehow she felt she had helped someone and she knew she wanted to do it again.

"Clara, you were wonderful!" Her sister was standing in front of her, out of breath with excitement.

"Yes, you were." Her mother beamed proudly at her.

As Clara took her seat, she basked in the praise from her family. She was surprised that some of the women in the room were lining up to try to talk to her. Clara was happy that things had gone so well. In spite of this, she felt sad. Why did she have to get it together after Jason left?

"Clara, look who's here!" Her sister exclaimed.

Clara looked up and saw Jason fighting his way through the women who were waiting to talk to her. She laughed at the sight of him being pushed and shoved by the women as he made his way through. Clara stood to her feet. "Hey ladies. Let that man through."

The women parted like the red sea and made a path for Jason to walk through.

Clara stood smiling as she waited for Jason. At the same time, she wondered what he was doing there.

After Jason walked through, the women once again crowded together to wait to talk to Clara.

"Well, Mister. What are you doing here?" Clara's heart thumped in her chest.

"Clara, I love you and I can't live one more day without you."

"Jason." Clara looked at him as if to remind him of their last conversation.

"Clara, I heard your speech. I heard what you said about issues from the past. I realize that I have some issues of my own. Things that I've been trying not to face. I never told you but my father kept a lot of secrets from my mother."

Clara wondered if Jason realized that he was standing in the midst of at least ninety women.

"My father had many women, Clara. He used to take me with him to visit these women."

"Jason, would you like to talk when I'm done?"

"Yes, and every day for the rest of our lives, but right now, I want to say that I never wanted to be like my father. But when you put me out I said, what the heck, I might as well go ahead and be like my old man." Jason shifted his weight from his right foot to his left, then standing flat-footed he continued, "Finding women to hang out with was easy. They all wanted to help me feel better but I realized that I didn't want that. It only made things worse."

Clara looked at him and fell in love all over again. Finally, she knew what real love felt like, honest and pure and perfect.

"Clara, I did some things while we were apart." Jason went on, "I can't undo them or take them back. But I can tell you that you're the only woman for me." He looked around him, seeming to notice the crowd of women for the first time. "That is, if you'll have me."

Clara smiled and gestured for him to come to her.

Jason walked over. He blushed when the women started laughing and clapping.

Then the room grew quiet.

Clara looked around at the women crowded around them. Then she looked into Jason's eyes.

"Jason, I love you and I do want to be with you. I forgive you for whatever happened while we were apart and I'm sorry for treating you the way I did." She reached out and took his hand. "I'm dealing with a lot of things right now that had me pretty messed up in the past. Let's just take things one day at a time, okay?"

"Okay." Jason smiled and blushed again as Clara kissed him lightly on the lips.

Nobody's Business Order Form

Use this convenient order form to order additional copies of
Nobody's Business

Please Print:

Name_____

Address_____

City_____ **State** _____

Zip Code _____

Phone (**)**_____

_____ copies of book @ $14.95 each $_____

Postage and handling @ $3.00 per book $_____

NJ residents add .90 tax per book $_____

Total amount enclosed $_____

Make checks payable to
Diligence Publishing Company

Send to Diligence Publishing Company
41 Watchung Plaza #239
Montclair, NJ 07042

Or visit us online at:
http://www.DPC-Books.com

Thank You!

Thank you for reading my first novel *Nobody's Business.*

I am sure that you have plenty of questions. So we have set up an interactive web page for all of the readers of Nobody's Business who want to stay in touch with the characters. At this website, you will be able to talk to other readers about *Nobody's Business*, ask the author questions and have them answered, and you may even be able to get in touch with Clara.

Stop by our website at www.DPC-Books.com to sign the guestbook and to find out how to check into the *Nobody's Business* interactive website. I look to see you there!

Thanks again for reading
Nobody's Business.

Rebecca Simmons
Diligence Publishing Company
41 Watchung Plaza #239
Montclair, NJ 07042
973-680-8438

www.DPC-Books.com

Also, if you are interested in finding out how to purchase a copy of the painting from Justine's office, please contact Audrey and Bill Swinson at 732-919-7088, or you can stop by their website at www.swinsonshowcaseppiart.com

Thanks again for reading Nobody's Business

About The Author

Rebecca Simmons is a life-long resident of New Jersey. She grew up in Newark and often talks about how reading books showed her the possibilities of a different life. She has been telling stories since she was ten years old. She would gather her brother and sisters and their friends around her at night and make up stories to entertain them. She loved the art of weaving tales almost as much as she enjoyed the looks on their faces as they gave her their full attention.

Rebecca is married with four children. She attended Rutgers University and University of Phoenix Online in pursuit of a Business Degree. She recently resigned from her position as a Senior Registered Associate at Merrill Lynch to pursue her dream of being a writer and a motivational speaker. She is thrilled to have fulfilled her dream of being a published author. Rebecca is already working on her second book and intends to write many more. Her main focus is relationships and she dreams of providing resources that will develop and improve relationships everywhere.

Rebecca is a member of The Cathedral International in Perth Amboy, New Jersey, where she and her husband serve on the executive committee of the marriage ministry. She is a member of AACC and affiliated with Several Sources in New Jersey. Her ultimate goal is to make a positive difference in the world, one life, one book, and one speech at a time.